Casting Shadows

Also by Sophie McKenzie

FALLING FAST

BURNING BRIGHT

GIRL, MISSING

SISTER, MISSING

MISSING ME

BLOOD TIES

BLOOD RANSOM

SIX STEPS TO A GIRL

THREE'S A CROWD

THE ONE AND ONLY

THE MEDUSA PROJECT 1: *THE SET-UP*

THE MEDUSA PROJECT 2: *THE HOSTAGE*

THE MEDUSA PROJECT WORLD BOOK DAY SPECIAL: *THE THIEF*

THE MEDUSA PROJECT 3: *THE RESCUE*

THE MEDUSA PROJECT 4: *HUNTED*

THE MEDUSA PROJECT 5: *DOUBLE-CROSS*

THE MEDUSA PROJECT 6: *HIT SQUAD*

Casting Shadows

SOPHIE McKENZIE

SIMON AND SCHUSTER

Acknowledgements: with thanks to Moira Young, Gaby Halberstam, Julie Mackenzie, Melanie Edge, Lou Kuenzler and Lily Kuenzler.

First published in Great Britain in 2013 by Simon and Schuster UK Ltd, a CBS company.

Simon & Schuster UK Ltd
1st Floor, 222 Gray's Inn Road, London WC1X 8HB

A CIP catalogue record for this book is available from the British Library.

PB ISBN: 978-0-85707-103-3
EBOOK ISBN: 978-0-85707-104-0

1 3 5 7 9 10 8 6 4 2

Printed and bound by CPI Group (UK) Ltd, Croydon CR0 4YY.

www.simonandschuster.co.uk
www.sophiemckenziebooks.com

For Venetia Gosling

1

Flynn and I sat at the table by the window, waiting. We were still at Café Yazmina, though my daytime shift had finished over an hour ago.

The window was open and a light breeze filtered in, cooling my face. The closer we got to Dad's arrival, the more churned up I felt. Flynn reached across the table and squeezed my hand. 'It's going to be fine,' he said.

I nodded, not feeling convinced. I fingered the tiny silver heart on the chain bracelet he'd given me.

'We'll help,' my friend Grace said from across the table.

'That's right.' Her boyfriend, James, sat beside her, his arm draped loosely across her shoulders.

I looked at them both, then at Flynn's determined face. Around us the café was filling up for dinner, despite the early hour. A large party had just walked in and the waiting staff were busy putting tables together to seat them.

'There's nothing to worry about,' Flynn said with a grin. 'James is even prepared to say I'm his role model.'

'Role model for being a git,' James grunted.

We all laughed. I felt the tension easing away from me. Maybe our plan *would* work. After all, Flynn had changed and Dad was reasonable – certainly a lot more reasonable than Mum. Plus, Flynn and I had been working up to this moment for weeks: what we were going to say and how we were going to say it.

Once Dad knew how much effort Flynn had put into dealing with his anger problems, he'd surely be happy for me to go out with him again.

'How long till your dad arrives?' Grace asked, twirling a lock of her blonde hair around her finger.

I checked the clock on the wall. It was almost 6.20 p.m. 'Ten minutes or so.' As I spoke, Yazmina – the owner of the café – bustled over, a huge presence in her flowing, glittery skirt and long, tasselled earrings. She smiled down at us then waved expansively at the room behind us. Her bangles jangled.

'We are very busy,' she drawled, flashing her white teeth in a big smile. 'River, I know you have finished your shift, and you are changed now into your own clothes, but might you help for a few minutes?'

I followed her gaze to the table across the room, where the people from the large party were sitting chatting to each other.

'Just to serve the meze . . . the starters,' Yazmina went on. 'Only for a few minutes. You will finish before your father arrives, yes?'

I hesitated. I didn't mind helping out at all, but I'd been so focused on what I was going to say to Dad that it was hard to adjust back into service mode.

'I'll do it.' Flynn stood up. 'If your dad arrives early, he'll see me working. That'll help make a good impression.'

I smiled at him gratefully and sat back in my chair as Yazmina glided away with Flynn following.

It was the end of June, a hot, close Friday evening. Flynn and I had been going out since last October. But back in January Flynn had hit his da and broken his nose. His da's a drunk who used to beat Flynn's mum and terrorise the rest of the family. After Flynn attacked his dad, his mum had gone back to her home in Ireland with Flynn and his sisters.

It was terrible being apart from each other and, at the beginning of March, Flynn had come back to London on his own. Since then he'd been working hard, sleeping on friends' sofas and studying in his spare time. He'd also been seeing a counsellor about his temper – that was my condition for going back out with him. Flynn hadn't liked the idea at first but he'd found a free service through his old school, where one of the tutors had also helped him organise everything he needed to take his exams.

And it had worked. I hadn't seen Flynn fly off the handle for almost three months. Well, I didn't see Flynn at all for the first few weeks – he insisted it was the only way to prove he had changed – though we'd sent each other texts most days. We started meeting up again at the very end of the Easter holidays and, once we'd seen each other, it was just too hard to keep apart. To be honest I think it helped me to know that Flynn was there, always ready to listen when I got bored of my revision or to give me a hug when I complained I was never going to pass Maths or Science.

I'd only been back at school for a few weeks before study leave started, after which my GCSEs kind of took over everything for a while. Flynn was perfect through that whole time. He always insisted I should do my work before we met up, revising hard for his own AS levels too. He never once overreacted or got angry about anything. I was impressed – and surprised, though I shouldn't have been. Flynn's the most determined person I've ever met. Once he decides to do something, nothing will stop him.

Still, I hated our relationship being secret. Mum

and Dad had forbidden us to contact each other back in January. As far as they were concerned, Flynn was still in Ireland. We'd kept his return ultra secret. Of our old friends, only James, Flynn's best friend, and Grace knew he was here – and we'd only told them about a month ago. Our plan was to introduce Flynn to Dad properly – they'd only met very briefly until now – then explain about his counselling sessions, his various jobs and his efforts to keep up with his schoolwork in the evenings. James and Grace were going to add their own character references.

Dad was such a forgiving old hippy, I couldn't believe he wouldn't accept Flynn back in my life. And once I had him on side, we'd go on and approach Mum.

James got up to go to the toilet. As he passed Flynn, he said something quietly. Flynn turned, bending closer to catch the whisper. His fringe flopped over his eyes and he grinned at whatever James was saying.

I stared, transfixed by his face. It was partly the way his nose sloped, the way his lips curved. But it was more than that too. Flynn's face was so mobile, so expressive. I never got tired of looking at it.

I watched Flynn stroll towards the kitchen. He moved with just a tiny hint of a swagger – all tall and lean and rangy and sure of himself.

'You really love him, don't you, River?' Grace said timidly.

I jumped. I'd forgotten she was still there. I'd forgotten, in fact, the whole café around us.

I blushed. 'He's really different now, Grace.' I turned to her. 'You can see that, can't you?'

Grace gave me a quick, shy nod but she turned away as she nodded, her sleek blonde bob swaying across her cheeks, hiding her face. It wasn't exactly a wholehearted endorsement but I didn't expect her to understand. Grace is lovely but she's never felt comfortable around Flynn. I think he's too intense for her. Too edgy.

I looked over again as Flynn re-emerged from the kitchen, a row of plates balanced along his arms. As he placed each one carefully on the table of eight, the rounded cut of the muscles on his upper arm showed for a second through his white shirt. It was crazy. I'd known him for nine months and my knees still buckled when I looked at him across a room. Flynn laid the last plate down and went back to the kitchen. Grace would never understand but it was precisely Flynn's intensity that I loved. I mean, he came back to London to be with me. He said – says – that I'm all that matters to him.

'Excuse me,' said a male voice impatiently.

I spun round. A middle-aged guy from one of the corner tables was standing in front of me, scowling.

I stared at him blankly.

'I heard the lady saying you worked here and I'd like some salt.' He said it slowly, in the sort of voice you might use on a really stupid person. 'There's none on our table and the other staff seem to be busy.'

'Sure,' I said, rising to my feet, ignoring the irritation I felt at his rude tone. 'I'll fetch some.'

I scuttled into the kitchen, almost colliding with Flynn on his way out. He was now carrying a basket of pitta bread in each hand.

'Hey, Riv.' He grinned at me. 'Slow down.'

The two male cooks were busy arguing on the far side of the kitchen. The scent of cardamom from the stew they were making wafted towards me.

'Slow down yourself,' I said, smiling back.

Flynn moved closer. 'Well, as you're here . . .' He drew even nearer, his eyes like gold discs in the bright, overhead kitchen light.

Irresistible.

I stood on tiptoe and kissed his mouth.

I'd meant to just brush his lips, to make it a light kiss, but once I felt him kiss me back I didn't want to stop. I put my arms round his neck and pulled him closer. He groaned. His hands were still full of the pitta baskets but I could hear the sound of bread dropping onto the floor. I smiled and kissed him harder, forgetting where we were. Forgetting the guys cooking in the corner of the kitchen. Forgetting all the people waiting outside in the café.

It was weird him not holding me while we kissed. Kind of sexy, actually. It made me feel more in control. I brought my hands down his back then let go. He pulled away, his forehead beaded with sweat.

Well, it *was* hot in the kitchen.

'River.' Yazmina's heavily accented voice pierced through me.

I jumped back guiltily and turned round. Yazmina was standing in the doorway, a half smile on her lips.

Behind her, his eyes wide with shock, stood Dad.

2

I froze.

A few long seconds passed. Then Yazmina gave a low chuckle. She stood back, holding the door through to the café open.

'Take the food out, Flynn,' she said.

Flynn didn't move. The cooks across the kitchen had stopped arguing and were watching us with interest.

I stared at Dad. His mouth had fallen open. 'River?' he said.

'Hello, Dad.'

'Hello, Mr Armstrong,' Flynn said. He sounded a little sullen but I knew he was just embarrassed. This was so *not* what we'd planned.

My heart raced. Nobody spoke, then Dad said, 'Hello again, Flynn.' His voice sounded tight and he wasn't smiling.

No, this was *awful*.

Yazmina sighed. 'Flynn,' she said firmly, looking down at the half-empty baskets of pitta bread in his hands. 'Please take the food outside.'

Flynn nodded. He glanced at me for a quick, desperate second, then strode away through the swing doors.

Yazmina raised her eyes at me. 'Perhaps you would pick up the bread on the floor, River,' she said, her eyes twinkling. She turned to Dad. 'If you're going to shout, River can show you up to my rooms.' Then she followed Flynn out into the café.

My face burning, I bent down and started picking up slices of pitta bread from the floor.

'River?' Dad sounded hoarse. 'I can't believe it, that . . . that was *Flynn*.'

I bit my lip, my chest tightening. 'Yes, Dad,' I said. I swallowed. 'I . . . we . . .'

My heart sank. All our careful planning had been completely pointless. I'd intended to soften Dad up before Flynn came to join us. But now . . . No way was Dad going to believe Flynn and I were taking it easy . . . that we hadn't even *seen* each other while he got started with his anger management counselling. Dad had just seen us kissing.

How embarrassing was that?

I stood up, pieces of bread in my hands.

Dad grabbed my arm. 'I thought he was in Ireland,' he said slowly. 'I thought . . .'

'I'm sorry.' I couldn't look him in the eye. I turned and walked over to the food waste bin in the corner. As I shoved the bits of bread inside it, I took a deep breath. What did I do now? It occurred to me that all I *could* do was ignore that kiss . . . carry on as originally planned. I turned back, taking in Dad's worried expression, the creases around his bright blue eyes, his tanned, worn face. I walked over and hugged him, breathing in the familiar smell of earth and incense from his shirt.

'Oh, Dad.' I looked up at him. 'I'm sorry . . . this wasn't how we planned . . . but Flynn's been back for a bit and—'

'How long?' Dad asked.

'Er, about three months, but—'

'*What?*' Dad said, horrified.

'He's *changed*, Dad,' I persisted. 'He's been seeing a counsellor. He's *totally* getting on top of all the anger stuff and—'

'Wait, River.' Dad frowned. 'Stop.'

'I know it's a shock but—'

'Slow down.' Dad shook his head. 'This is serious, River. You promised your mum and me that you weren't going to see Flynn again. Does *she* know he's back from Ireland?'

I wrinkled up my nose. 'No. I wanted to tell *you*

11

first, Dad. She and Flynn don't get on. But you're . . . you . . .'

'So when did he get in touch?'

I felt my shoulders sag. Why was Dad insisting on dragging the conversation down to all these details?

I looked up at him. His eyes were tender but wary. And there was something else in his expression too. Something closer to anger. That wasn't like Dad, he's the most laid-back man on the planet.

At that moment the swing doors burst open and Flynn strode back in. 'Hi,' he said awkwardly.

He stood for a second, gazing at me, then he turned to Dad, a determined look on his face.

'There's a corner table out there if you want it, Mr Armstrong,' he said. He brushed back his hair self-consciously. 'For two, I mean,' he added.

I blinked. I'd never heard Flynn speak so . . . so deferentially. His whole face was tense, but he lowered his eyes as Dad stared at him. My heart went out to him. He was trying so hard to get my dad to like him. And all for me. Without thinking, I reached out my hand and took his.

Flynn shot me a swift grin.

'I think we'll go somewhere else, actually,' Dad said in the stoniest voice I'd ever heard him use.

I could feel Flynn's hand tensing in mine. I gave it a warning squeeze, then let go.

'That's fine, Dad,' I said. I glanced at Flynn. His eyes were dark gold. I caught a flash of his old temper and shivered. 'It's okay,' I said. I don't know if I was talking to Flynn or to Dad or to myself. 'It's going to be okay.'

'Come on, River.' Dad held open the door out to the café.

I tore my eyes away from Flynn and walked through. As I headed for the door that led outside I could hear the man who'd spoken to me earlier complaining he still had no salt. Beyond him, I caught a glimpse of James and Grace, their mouths gaping with shock. So much for our plan to big-up Flynn. Bitter tears welled in my eyes.

Dad was lost in thought as we walked along Holloway Road to where his beaten-up old car was parked. My pulse raced as I tried to work out what to say next. All I'd wanted tonight was for Dad to realise Flynn had changed, so that he wouldn't mind us going back out together.

But now, no way was Dad going to get his head around the idea of us dating again. He couldn't even seem to get his head around unlocking his car. We stood on the pavement beside it while he fumbled in his pockets for the key, clearly not concentrating on what he was doing.

'Dad?' I said. 'What . . . where are we going?'

Dad stared round at me as if he'd forgotten I was there. 'I want you to come up to the commune with me,' he said. 'For the weekend, so we can talk properly.'

I frowned. This wasn't one of my scheduled days to visit Dad. He was just popping over to see me after a meeting with one of the commune's organic vegetable clients. I hadn't actually been to the commune for several weeks now, not since before my GCSE exams, though I'd agreed with Mum and Dad ages ago that I'd spend my school holidays there.

I didn't want to go. I'd planned to see Flynn this weekend – we were going to go to the park with Grace and James tomorrow afternoon, then to see a movie in the evening.

'But I don't have any stuff with me,' I said.

Dad shook his head. 'We can stop off at your mum's. Pick up what you need.' He paused. 'I want to talk to her anyway.'

My heart thudded. 'Dad, please don't tell her about Flynn.' I gripped his arm. 'Please. She'll be so mad.'

'River.' Dad rolled his eyes. 'I don't think you appreciate how . . . how let down I feel. You promised us you wouldn't have anything to do with that boy. That was the condition of letting you stay with your mother during term time, remember?'

I nodded.

'And now, to find out you're still involved with him all these months later. It's . . . I don't know what to say, what to think.'

'We did break up,' I said, anxiety clutching at my throat. 'And I told Flynn I wouldn't go back out with him unless he did something about his temper and he *has*. Like I told you, he's been seeing a counsellor. And he's got a job – three jobs, actually. *And* he worked really hard for his exams.'

Dad stared at me. I couldn't tell what he was thinking. I wanted to tell him how much I loved Flynn, how being apart from him before had nearly killed me. But I couldn't say it. I looked away, my face burning.

Behind me, I could hear Dad unlocking the car door. I scurried round to the other side and slid into the passenger seat.

We drove off in silence.

3

A few hours later I was sitting alone, on the bed in the little storeroom off Dad's living room in his and Gemma's commune apartment. It was where I usually slept when I stayed with them – unless my brother, Stone, came too. Then one of us had to sleep on the couch in the living room. I checked my phone again. The signal was always weak here but at least there *was* a signal. After we'd left Mum's and begun the long drive up to the commune, I'd texted Flynn and told him what had happened and he'd messaged back to say he'd call me at ten thirty.

I felt so lonely, so miserable without him.

I sighed and lay back on the bed. Dad had, of course, told Mum about Flynn. And Mum had, predictably, gone ballistic.

Ten more minutes passed. Flynn would be calling soon. I decided to go down to the kitchen, maybe get a drink. I had shut myself away as soon as we arrived, so I hadn't seen anyone who lived here yet. I was hoping to avoid the other residents. I took off my shoes and trotted down the stone steps, my socks silent but slippery against their smoothness. As I padded along the corridor to the kitchen, I heard Dad's voice.

'I couldn't believe the way she was . . . the way she . . . God, she was really kissing him.' He let out a big sigh.

'She's sixteen, love.' That was Gemma. 'Seventeen in a few months. She's not a baby.'

'I know,' Dad groaned. 'It's just it's hard, thinking about . . . you know . . .'

I shrank back against the stone wall of the corridor, my heart racing.

'Isn't the important thing how River feels? And also *how* it happens?' Gemma said gently. 'From what you said it sounds as if he was very respectful to you.'

Dad said something in a low voice that I couldn't catch.

'Okay,' Gemma said, 'but there were reasons why he attacked his dad. And lots of teenage boys get a bit out of control. He's never hurt *River*. And everyone deserves a second chance, don't they?'

Yes. I nodded, out in the corridor. My heart surged with affection for Gemma.

17

And then my phone rang. The sound filled the corridor. Chairs scraped back across the stone floor in the kitchen as I fled back towards the stairs. I answered the call as I panted up them, two at a time.

'River?' Flynn sounded concerned. 'You okay?'

'Yeah.' I tore into the little bedroom and collapsed onto the bed.

We talked for a few minutes. I kept my eyes on the door, but Dad and Gemma hadn't followed me. I could tell Flynn was upset that Dad was being so heavy about us seeing each other. He was trying hard to keep things light, to reassure me, but the tightness in his voice was unmistakeable. And I felt the same way.

We said we loved each other and rang off. I still felt troubled. I put my head in my hands. A rap on the door. Then Gemma poked her head round. 'River?' she said.

I looked up at her, my lips trembling. She smiled and walked over to me, scooping me into a hug. Tears welled up as she held me. She smelled like my dad – her clothes slightly musty with a whiff of incense, but on her the smell was lighter, more flowery somehow.

Gemma's not much bigger than me, really Completely different from Mum. She's got long black hair and, when you don't know her, she comes across as very gentle and shy. But she's a strong person. She and Dad lost their baby earlier in the year. I know it really upset them, especially Gemma, but she hasn't let it make her all bitter or mean. Dad adores her. It suddenly struck me that if anyone could persuade him to accept me and Flynn being together it was her.

'He's a good person,' I wept. 'He's really changed. He just needs people to believe in him.'

Gemma stroked my hair. 'I know, sweetheart,' she said.

'And I'm prepared to give him a chance.' I looked up. Dad was standing in the doorway, gazing at me. 'But there's one condition.'

I nodded eagerly, disentangling myself from Gemma's arms. 'What?'

Dad pursed his lips. 'I want to get to know him first. I want Flynn to come and spend the rest of the weekend here on the commune with you, me and Gemma.'

'Okay.' I frowned. 'But it's Friday night already . . . how is Flynn going to get here?'

'We'll pick him up from the station tomorrow. Tell him to get on a train to arrive by midday. I'll cover his fare.'

My heart was in my mouth as we waited at the station the next morning. Dad looked pretty tense too. As the train pulled in, I fingered the phone in my pocket. I was half expecting Flynn to call and tell me he couldn't face the interrogation he was bound to be given. Our last kiss flashed into my head. We'd have to be so careful about what we did in front of my dad. It was obvious that for all his liberal talk about human beings needing to love each other more, he was totally freaked out by the idea of me really loving someone myself.

The train stopped. I held my breath, waiting for Flynn to appear. He'd seemed so much calmer since he'd been seeing his counsellor, but he would be under enormous pressure coming face to face with Dad and having to spend time at the commune – a place he usually referred to disparagingly as the drop-out centre. Suppose he lost his temper with someone? Some of the people here were fairly odd and, if not drop-outs, certainly alternative in their approach to life.

Suppose he lost his temper with Dad?

The doors opened and Flynn stepped out onto the sunny platform. He loped along, looking around for us. I could tell he was uncertain of himself . . . there was something awkward in the hunch of his shoulders and the way his hands were stuffed into his pockets.

'There he is.' I hurried over, Dad at my side.

Flynn turned and saw us. His eyes – bright green in the sunlight – lit up as he looked at me. I had always adored how expressive his face was but now, for the first time, I was grateful that he was making his feelings so obvious. The love that shone from his eyes was exactly what I wanted Dad to see.

But how would he act with Dad himself?

We reached each other. Flynn leaned over and gave me a sedate kiss on the cheek. Then he turned to Dad and held out his hand.

'Hello, Mr Armstrong,' he said smoothly, all traces of his earlier awkwardness completely evaporating as he spoke. 'I'm sorry we didn't get a chance to talk properly the other day. It's a pleasure to finally spend some time with you. I know River loves you very much and, as I love her more than anything in the world, it's important to me that you know my intentions to her are entirely honourable.'

Entirely honourable?

I realised my mouth had fallen open and closed it. Flynn sounded like something out of a different century – and way older than his years. I was guessing that he had rehearsed that speech to Dad before arriving. He would certainly never talk in such a formal way normally. Still, he had made everything he'd said sound effortlessly natural and, more important, completely sincere.

Dad looked even more shocked than me as he shook Flynn's hand. Not surprising, really. All he'd heard about Flynn for the past five months was that he was hot-tempered to the point of violence. He couldn't possibly have expected this level of charm, maturity and manners.

'Good to see you too, Flynn,' Dad said. 'The car's this way.'

As we followed him out to the car, Flynn slipped his arm around my shoulders. I leaned into him and he lowered his face to whisper in my ear.

'How am I doing?' he said softly.

I looked up, into his eyes. Didn't he know how well he was coming across? He was trying so hard – and all so we could be together. I'd never loved him more. I smiled, reaching up to whisper back.

'Ace, I think Dad likes you already.'

After the fifteen-minute drive to the commune, I was *sure* Dad liked him. Flynn had continued with his charm offensive. He answered all Dad's questions about his jobs and his A levels politely and with a meek respectfulness I'd only ever seen him display at the gym where he worked, Goldbar's.

As soon as Dad sat back, clearly relaxing in the face of Flynn's good manners, Flynn asked a few questions of his own. Simple, interested questions

22

about the commune – how it worked and how many people lived there.

A few minutes later we arrived. I took Flynn's hand as we went into the kitchen via the back door. Flynn looked around, taking in the big stone floor and huge Aga stove. I wondered what he was thinking. The kitchen looked good – clean and warm and inviting in the morning sunshine that flooded in through the long window near the table. Still, compared to Mum's house with its fitted cupboards and stainless steel appliances, it was all quite basic.

'Hi, River!' It was Ros, one of my favourite residents, coming in from the garden. I liked Ros a lot. She was outgoing and funny and always treated me like a grown-up. 'And this must be Flynn?' Ros said, striding over with her arm outstretched.

Flynn shook her hand.

'*Very* attractive, River.' Ros winked in my direction.

I blushed. Flynn rolled his eyes but he was smiling.

Dad cleared his throat. 'Why don't you show Flynn round for a bit, River?' he said. 'Meet back here for lunch in half an hour?'

I nodded and tugged Flynn through the kitchen door. We wandered along the corridor. Flynn was moving slowly, gazing at the bare plaster on the walls. I showed him the two communal rooms – one with three large sofas and a huge fireplace in the centre. The other was smaller, full of books and magazines and two long desks.

'That's where Stone and I do our homework when we stay here,' I said nervously.

Flynn's eyes were sharp, soaking it all up. I swallowed. Looking at it fresh like this I was horribly aware of how tatty the whole place was. It really could do with a lick of paint – and some of the upholstery on the sofas was fraying badly. I knew Flynn would never look down on people for not having much money, but I was worried he might see the shabbiness of the commune as proof that the residents lacked drive and ambition, just like he'd always suspected.

I pointed along the corridor to the doors that led to two of the private apartments. 'John and Julia live on the left,' I explained. 'And Ros is opposite.' I glanced at him, feeling nervous. 'What did you make of her?'

Flynn shrugged. 'Seemed okay,' he said.

I nodded. 'Ros is cool, actually. She used to be an actor.'

'Yeah?' Flynn turned his attention to the abstract paintings that hung along the wall. I watched him taking them in. He was a brilliant actor himself, of course. That was how we'd met, last autumn, acting in *Romeo and Juliet* at his school.

I led him up the big stone stairs. At least upstairs was carpeted, even if the carpets were threadbare.

'There are two flats at this end.' I indicated them in turn: the small studio that belonged to the nerdy IT guy who kept himself to himself and the largest apartment in the commune which, as far as I knew, was still empty.

Flynn nodded absently. 'So where are we staying?' he said.

I led him along the building to Dad and Gemma's apartment. The door opened into a fair-sized living area – cosy and messy with throws over the couches, and shelves heaving with books and rows of plants around the huge window. I pointed to the two doors on the left. 'That's their bedroom and the bathroom,' I said.

'What's in there?' Flynn indicated the door on the opposite wall.

'That's the "storeroom-cum-spare room",' I said.

Flynn grinned at me and pushed open the door. It was its usual mess. The camp bed was made up with a white duvet and someone, Gemma presumably, had placed a vase of sweet pea flowers on the window ledge. Planks of wood, piles of boxes containing old magazines, papers of all kinds and scraps of fabric littered the floor at the base of the opposite wall.

'Dad's always saying he means to clear this room out,' I said. 'But he's busy outside most of the time.'

Flynn strode over to the little window above the bed. He'd sneered so often at the idea of the commune, where people came together to share their resources and work at being as self-sufficient as possible. What would he make of the reality?

I followed him over to the window. He was looking out over the vegetable garden, which lay to the right of the kitchen and the two fields beyond. The yard with the hens and the goat was out of sight from here, as was the barn which was hidden from view by the big oak tree at the bottom of the east field. The sun shone brightly in a clear blue sky.

'What do you think?' I said, unable to stand it any longer.

I held my breath, waiting for his reply. I wasn't sure why but everything suddenly seemed to ride on Flynn's answer.

4

'I think the place is beautiful,' Flynn said at last, beaming at me across the storeroom. The smile lit up his face, already bathed in the sunshine flooding in from outside. He suddenly looked much younger than before, like a child just landed in a sweet shop. 'Almost as beautiful as you.'

He put his hands on my arms and stared at me for a second. I held my breath, wanting him to kiss me so badly I could hardly stand. Then he grinned again and strode away to the door.

'Show me outside,' he said.

We went downstairs and I walked him past the hens then down through both fields. There were Jacob sheep in the second. Flynn was fascinated by their black and white wool and curling horns. He said he'd never seen a real live sheep close to before.

We kissed in the apple orchard. I'd been there a million times – it was just about my favourite place in the commune, especially at this time of year, with the trees full of budding fruit and the sweet scent of the wild flowers in the air.

As we strolled back, hand in hand, the gong for lunch sounded.

'What's that?' Flynn asked.

I gulped, my anxieties flooding back. I wasn't sure who would be here today – people were often out at weekends – but it was hard to imagine Flynn sitting down to any kind of communal meal with strangers. I prayed that Gemma or Ros had been cooking. At least then I could be sure the food would be good.

'It's another chance to make a positive impression,' I said lightly.

'Right.' Flynn grinned. 'No problem.'

To my relief, the kitchen wasn't too full when we arrived. Dad and Gemma were already sitting down at the long table, laid with the usual mismatched bowls and spoons. Ros was next to Gemma with the nerdy IT guy opposite. They looked up as we walked in.

Dad beckoned for me and Flynn to sit down. I had butterflies in my stomach but Flynn was as charming as he had been earlier and my anxieties soon eased.

After a few minutes, John and Julia hurried in from the utility room with two large loaves of home-made bread and a tureen of soup. John, who is kind of annoyingly full of himself, was explaining how they'd made the soup in great detail.

'. . . so then we added a pinch of – genius touch, I don't mind saying – *tarragon* . . .'

Flynn and I sat down with the others. To my relief, the food was excellent. Everything seemed relaxed but, as we ate, I shot Flynn a quick look. He was eating fast, wolfing down his soup. I could tell from the way his knuckles were white as they gripped his spoon that, despite his easy manner, he was finding this whole meal a strain. He didn't like joining in *anything*, not even with people our age at school. He'd only done the school play we'd both been in because the drama teacher had insisted. I could only imagine how hard this big sit-down lunch was for him.

'So what d'you think of the place, Flynn?' Dad asked.

Everyone looked at Flynn. I held my breath.

'I like it,' he said. 'It's beautiful, especially outside – the sheep are amazing – and . . . it's huge.'

Silence fell around the table.

Ros chuckled. 'Still, size isn't everything, ha-ha!'

I looked down at the table, blushing. The nerdy IT guy said something under his breath to Gemma and she rolled her eyes.

Flynn looked awkward again. I put my hand over his, trying to reassure him that everything was still okay. The silver heart from my bracelet felt cool against my skin. Flynn looked up at me, the gaze from his greeny-gold eyes all soulful.

'It's fine,' I mouthed. 'Everyone loves you.'

Flynn leaned over, his lips brushing my ear, sending shivers down my spine. 'I only care that you love me.'

'Hey, guys, share the joke,' Ros said.

I smiled over at her. 'Nothing,' I said.

Flynn smiled too, then asked more questions about the commune. He found out things I'd never known, such as why some of the sheep had six horns, and the way everyone joining had to make a down payment as investment into the group, then commit to working a certain number of hours every week.

'We try to make the best use of everyone's skills,' Dad said, warming to one of his favourite topics.

'So Gemma cooks, Ros makes everyone laugh and John tells everyone what to do,' I said.

Everyone laughed, even John.

After lunch, Dad took me and Flynn out to the east field to mend a fence. Flynn was eager to learn and totally cooperative, doing everything Dad told him. By the time we went in to wash for supper, they were chatting away like they'd known each other forever.

Gemma had been cooking and the kitchen was filled with the scent of curry spices. Flynn and I made ourselves mugs of tea and took them down to the apple orchard while Dad and Ros laid the table.

'You seem so relaxed here,' I said, as Flynn leaned against a tree. 'Not when we were eating with everyone so much, but here . . . outside . . . Do you really like it?'

It was twilight and the birds were singing out. Above our heads, the sky was shot through with swirls of pink and orange. Flynn took a gulp of tea.

'I like your dad and Gemma,' he said. 'And that Ros is a laugh. And . . . and I like how much space there is outside and I like the way everyone knows what they're supposed to do and just gets on and does it.'

I nodded, surprised he was sounding so positive.

'So you don't think the people here are drop-outs anymore?' I said.

'Man, they're total drop-outs,' Flynn said with a grin. 'I mean, I get the concept but it's all a bit . . .' he paused, searching for the right word, 'I dunno, it must get a bit dull just living here day in, day out.'

'Unambitious?' I said. This was a word my mum often threw at my dad.

31

'Yeah, I guess.' Flynn drained his tea, then drew me towards him. 'Never mind all that. How much time do we have till dinner?'

The evening meal passed as easily as lunchtime had. Flynn was offered – and refused – a beer. I noticed Dad raise his eyebrows when Flynn announced that he never drank alcohol. I could tell Dad wasn't sure whether to believe him.

'It's true, Dad,' I said. 'Flynn never has anything to drink when we're out.'

'Why's that?' asked John imperiously. 'Bit odd for a guy your age, isn't it?'

Flynn turned to him. I could tell he was dying to snap out some snarky remark but he didn't. He waited a second before replying, then he gave the same response he'd given when I'd first asked him that question months ago.

'I don't like drunks,' he said.

I knew – and I was guessing Dad and Gemma did too – that this was a reference to Flynn's alcoholic father. My eyes flitted to the place on Flynn's shoulder, hidden by his shirt, where his dad had cut him years ago with a glass bottle, leaving a long, jagged scar.

I looked around the table, praying that nobody asked any further questions. Flynn's father was definitely one topic I didn't want us to get into. Both John and Ros looked like they wanted to know more, but something about Flynn's steel-eyed glare stopped them.

We went up to Dad and Gemma's rooms as soon as we'd washed up after the meal. Dad had made it clear Flynn was to sleep on the sofa, while I took my usual bed in the storeroom. We sat and played a game on my phone for an hour or so, then we went for a walk outside. Flynn was sweet and tender and delighted that I kept saying I was sure Dad liked him.

I fell asleep as soon as my head touched my pillow, my heart full of hope for a future where it would be okay for me and Flynn to be together.

The next morning, Dad announced a man and his son would be coming to look at the empty commune apartment. I didn't pay much attention. They'd had a few viewers in the past couple of months but the apartment was large and nobody, so far, had wanted it.

Dad and I dropped Flynn at the station just before lunch. He had to get back home for his job at Goldbar's, the gym and boxing club. As he was currently staying in the owner's spare room, he felt he couldn't really ask to take the shift off. He had been brilliant all morning, helping to prune the apple trees, a job that had to be done every June and which I always enjoyed. When he left, Ros and Gemma both gave him big hugs and even John shook his hand with a warm smile and a 'good to meet you, young man'. At the station itself, Flynn said something quietly in Dad's ear before turning and walking off to the platform.

Dad said very little as we drove back to the commune. After a few minutes, I couldn't bear it any longer. 'So what did you think?' I blurted out. 'Are you okay with us seeing each other again?'

Dad said nothing, just changed gears in the car.

'Listen, Dad,' I went on. 'When you and Mum said not to see Flynn back in January, you were right. He was out of control then. But he's changed. He's making a real effort now. Trying not to—'

'I know, River,' Dad interrupted. 'I get it.'

'What did he say when he left?' My heart was in my mouth.

Dad stared at the road ahead. 'Exactly what you've been saying . . . that he's changed . . . that he's sorry for not making more effort before . . . that he loves you.'

My throat felt swollen. 'And?' I breathed. 'Does that mean you're okay with us being together?'

'Not really.' Dad gazed over at me. 'I mean, I'm still prepared to think about it but like I told Flynn when we were pruning, I'm very wary, because of his temper. I said I was sure that if he looked at the situation from my point of view he would understand.'

My eyes widened. I had no idea Dad had spoken like that to Flynn earlier and could just imagine Flynn's angry response.

'What did Flynn say?' I whispered.

Dad turned the car onto the road that led to the commune.

'He said yes, that he did understand, but that he was still determined to show me he had changed.' Dad looked across at me again. 'He said he was changing because of you . . . for you.'

5

After lunch, I spent the afternoon reading in the apple orchard. It was another beautiful day and, after the tension of Flynn's visit, I could feel myself totally relaxing in the sunshine. By 3 p.m. the wind died completely and I was sweltering hot, even in the shade. I took off my shoes and rolled the waist of my skirt right over, so the material was up at the top of my thighs, not flapping around my legs. It didn't help much but I didn't have a bikini here and I didn't want to strip to my underwear with so many people around.

I fell asleep under one of the trees, waking with a start to the sound of a breaking twig. A boy about my age was standing beside the tree opposite.

I sat bolt upright and yanked at my skirt, tugging it down over my legs. The boy's startled eyes followed my hands and when I glanced back up at him a flush was creeping over his pale cheeks.

'Who are you?' I said.

'Hi.' He offered me an embarrassed smile. 'I'm Leo. My dad and I are visiting today, looking at the spare apartment.' His eyes were a pale, clear blue, startling against his very fair skin. He was actually quite good-looking, but there was something awkward about his manner – like he wasn't comfortable in himself.

I scrambled to my feet, pulling my skirt right down. Dad had mentioned earlier that people would be coming to view the spare apartment.

'This is the apple orchard,' I said, rather unnecessarily as the trees we were standing under were groaning with tiny, unripe apples.

'Do you live here?' Leo asked. He wasn't tall – maybe just a few centimetres taller than me – and his blond hair fell in soft waves. He wore nice clothes, I noted. Cool jeans and a T-shirt with a target pattern on the front.

'No, I'm just visiting my dad.' I paused. I knew I should have given my name, but I'd always hated saying it to people for the first time. It probably made me come across as aloof, even arrogant, but it was so embarrassing when people didn't hear properly what I'd said and I had to repeat it or spell it out for them.

'You're River?' Leo said.

'Yes,' I said, grateful that he had already heard of me. 'So what do you think of the place? Does your dad like it?'

'I think so,' he said. 'It's a bit weird but . . .' He tailed off and stared at the ground.

'Yeah,' I said, remembering how odd the whole commune set-up had seemed when Dad had first moved here. 'You get used to it.'

Leo nodded. 'D'you know what Norton Napier College is like?'

'Er, sorry, never heard of it.'

'It's the local sixth form college,' Leo explained. 'If we do move here that's where I'll be going next term.'

I shook my head. I hadn't even known there *was* a sixth form college near here.

There was a short pause.

'So is it just you and your dad?' I said.

Leo nodded again. 'Yeah.' He shuffled from foot to foot. 'My mum died last year.'

'Oh.' I didn't know what to say. 'I'm sorry.'

Leo looked embarrassed. 'Dad went a bit mad after,' he said. 'Started going out all the time. Bringing people back in the middle of the night. Getting drunk. So dull might be good for a bit.'

I nodded slowly. I felt a little uncomfortable. I'm not a big one for lots of phony small talk, but there was something a bit desperate about the way Leo had launched into his life story after just a few seconds.

'Sorry.' Leo blushed again, as if he was reading my mind. 'Too much information, yeah?'

'It's fine,' I said, hoping he hadn't thought I was rude. 'Sounds like you've been through a lot, you know . . .'

'Hey, River!' Dad was calling. He sounded quite a way off, probably back at the house.

I made a face at Leo. 'Better go,' I said, with an apologetic shrug.

I sauntered out of the orchard and across the field. I could see Dad now, standing outside the kitchen door waving at me. As I got near to the house, Dad disappeared inside. Something made me look over my shoulder just in time to catch a glimpse of blond hair vanishing behind one of the apple trees.

I walked into the kitchen, where a tall man with a bit of a paunch and long grey hair tied back in a ponytail was deep in conversation with John. That must be Leo's dad. He glanced up as I came in and Dad introduced us.

'So, how are you finding the place?' Dad asked.

'I love it,' Leo's dad said with a beaming smile. 'Just hope the boy likes it too.'

I wondered what it would be like to visit the

commune if Leo and his dad moved in and there was someone my own age here for once. Leo had seemed nice enough, if a little bit intense. But then he was bound to be intense if his mum had died recently.

Dad said he would drive me home after we'd had a cup of tea and 'a chat' so we went up to his and Gemma's apartment for a bit of privacy.

'Sit down, River,' Dad said.

I perched on the edge of the couch, wondering what was coming next. Gemma set a steaming mug of tea in front of me. She rested her hand lightly on my shoulder then disappeared into the bedroom.

I looked across at Dad. His blue eyes were crinkled with concern. I swallowed. It felt like there was a dull weight pressing down on my chest. 'Dad?' I said.

'I'm not going to forbid you to see him,' Dad said.

Hope fluttered inside me. Did he mean that? What about Mum? Was he prepared to try and convince her Flynn was okay?

'I just want you to be careful.' Dad rubbed his forehead. 'You'll be spending the whole summer here anyway, and obviously Flynn will be working, so there won't be so many opportunities . . . ' He tailed off.

I hesitated, a confusion of emotions running

around my head. Was Dad only saying we could be together because he thought that spending the summer apart would be enough to break us up? Did he really still not get it?

I crossed the room and gazed out of the window. Leo, his father and John were crossing the east field. Leo lagged behind the others, a lonely figure ignored by the two men who were deep in conversation. There was something in his slouching, unhappy walk that I totally related to.

My breath caught in my throat as a brilliant idea struck me. *No.* It was mad. And yet it solved every problem in one fell swoop. But would Dad go for it?

'Dad?'

He looked up, his eyes all blue and crinkly against his tanned face.

'I've got an idea,' I said. 'Maybe I could come to school here this autumn. I mean, Mum's already made it clear she'd rather I stayed with you over the holidays. And there's a sixth form place – Norton Napier College – just up the road.'

Dad blinked. His shirt was untucked and the sleeves rolled halfway up his arms. He unrolled them and rerolled them as I waited for a reply.

'You don't want to stay on at your own school for sixth form?' he said.

I shook my head. It wasn't that I didn't like it at

41

Langton but I had only really ever had two good friends there – Grace, who I saw outside school anyway, mostly when we doubled-dated with Flynn and James, and Emmi, who I'd hardly seen for ages because her boyfriend, Alex, and Flynn didn't get on at all. I would miss Grace, but I was certain we'd stay in touch wherever I lived. On the other hand, I was fairly sure I'd be seeing less of Emmi in the future, whatever happened. I hadn't even told her I was going out with Flynn again.

I turned to Dad. 'I could move in here – into the storeroom. We could clear it out. That's if . . . if Gemma didn't mind.'

'No . . . I . . . I don't think she'd mind . . . but . . .' Dad frowned. 'I don't understand, River. I mean, you coming to live here is one conversation. But we were talking about you and Flynn, which is another. So—'

'I know.' I nodded eagerly. This was the whole point. 'Flynn could move in too,' I said.

Dad's eyes widened. '*What?*'

'We could both live here,' I went on breathlessly, the whole plan unfolding in my mind as I spoke. 'I'll be here, which you wanted for the summer anyway. And Flynn too. It will be a fresh start for him. He can go to a counsellor at Gemma's therapy place. Come September, we can both go to the sixth form college. He can earn his rent here doing extra chores. You should have seen him last year. He did about four jobs after school, trying to help his mum and—'

Dad held up his hand. 'It's out of the question, River,' he said. 'What about Flynn's mum? What about yours? She'll never agree to him living here too.'

'But you said it was okay for us to be back together.' I flew across the room and sat down beside him. 'Flynn's mother would be pleased if he had somewhere proper to stay. And Mum doesn't get on with Flynn *that* badly.'

This last point was a total lie and Dad knew it. Mum had disliked Flynn from the first moment she met him last autumn. She thought he was rude and moody and aggressive – not to mention a bad influence on me.

Dad raised his eyebrows. 'You and I both know that your mother isn't exactly Flynn's biggest fan.' A small smile crept across Dad's face. 'I told him that was one thing we had in common – as well as you, of course.'

I stared at him. 'But *you* liked him, didn't you?' I said, sensing it was true.

Dad turned away. 'In spite of myself, I did,' he admitted. 'I mean, I could see how angry he is but there's this hurt kid there too, who has had a really raw deal in life. It's very rare for someone his age, who's lived through what he's lived through, to be prepared to face up to the consequences like he's trying to do.'

'Oh, Dad.' My heart was hammering. 'So it could work then. I mean, you'd like *me* to live here, wouldn't you?'

Dad wiped his forehead. 'Of course I would, but we've already established that your mum won't go for it, so . . .'

'Mum can't stop me living here if it's what I want,' I said. 'It was actually her idea, remember? She was on the verge of making me come here last term.'

Dad's eyes widened. 'That was only because she didn't like you being with Flynn, she . . . *we* . . . said you would have to come here if you refused to stop seeing him.'

'But Flynn's changed,' I insisted. 'Come on, Dad, at least say you'll think about it.'

'No, River.' Dad crossed his arms. 'There's no way.'

I glared at him, fury boiling up inside me.

'But Flynn doesn't have anywhere else to go,' I said. 'You heard him this weekend. He's living on people's sofas and holding down three jobs *and* he just took his AS levels. He managed that okay because there was study leave for weeks and *now* it's all right because it's almost the summer holidays, but how is he going to cope with A2s next year?'

'I know how hard he's worked, Riv—'

'It's not fair. He got all A*s in his GCSEs and he's predicted top grades for the ASs but he says the work now is much harder. And he can't stay on people's sofas forever.'

'Where would he stay here?' Dad said. 'There's no room. Stone comes every other weekend and we can't permanently give up our living room.'

'He'll share the storeroom with me,' I said.

'No.' The word shot out of Dad's mouth like a bullet. 'No, I've said "no" and that's an end to it.'

I stared at him. I'd never seen him so emphatic about anything. So much for that laid-back exterior of his. Scratch the surface and he was really just like Mum underneath.

I stood up and backed away from him. 'You're not giving him a chance, Dad. He doesn't have anywhere else to go.'

'That's not my problem,' Dad snapped.

I gasped. I'd never heard Dad sound so harsh.

'You hypocrite.' Tears bubbled up into my eyes. 'You live here preaching all that rubbish about helping people and finding peace with the universe and here's someone you could actually help and you won't lift a finger for him, even . . .' I choked

45

back the sobs that were rising through my chest and into my throat... 'even though he means *everything* to me.'

I turned and stomped out of the room, downstairs and out to the car. I leaned against the metal, hot on my back, and gazed out towards the yard with the hen house and to the apple orchard beyond. Earlier it had seemed idyllic, but right now it felt like a prison.

6

I was so angry I didn't speak to Dad for the rest of
my time at the commune. He tried to talk during the
journey home but I just stared out of the car window
the whole way. When we got back to Mum's he
followed me indoors. I went straight upstairs but I
could still hear him and Mum discussing me and
Flynn in the kitchen. Mum's voice was raised – she
seemed to be blaming Dad for me thinking that
living with Flynn was even a remote possibility.
Normally when she picked on Dad I'd try and
defend him. But, at that moment, I was glad she was
giving him a hard time, he deserved it. I mean, I
understood they wanted to protect me but I was
going to be seventeen in a few months. When were
they going to realise I was old enough to make my
own decisions? I was totally fed up with them trying
to run my life.

I knew Flynn was still at work, so I called Grace

from my bedroom. We talked for a while, then agreed to meet up. I got changed, ready to go out, then went downstairs. Dad was *still* there. He came out of the kitchen when he heard me on the stairs.

'River—?'

'I'm going out,' I said.

Mum appeared at his shoulder. Her lips were pressed together in a thin line. 'River?' she began.

'The answer is yes, I probably will see Flynn later,' I said. 'So you'll both just have to deal with it.'

And I walked out, slamming the front door behind me.

I knew I was being hard on them but right then I didn't care.

I went round to Grace's. James was already there and Flynn joined us an hour or so later.

We talked about what it would be like to live together at the commune. Though Grace didn't say it, I could see she was wondering why I'd want to go so far away from all my friends.

Flynn had other objections.

'It'd be great, Riv,' he said with a shrug. 'But there'd still be drawbacks. We'd have your dad breathing down our necks all the time – and all that we're-saving-the-planet-by-eating-our-own-hens rubbish would definitely wind me up.'

'Do they really eat the hens on the commune?' Grace asked, looking appalled.

'No.' I grinned, catching Flynn's eye. 'The hens are just for eggs. They don't eat any meat on the commune.'

'See what I mean?' Flynn shook his head. 'Veggie nightmare.'

'I wouldn't survive a week without a burger,' James mused.

'You can tell.' Flynn poked him in the stomach.

James laughed good-naturedly. I smiled, feeling more relaxed than I had done in days. I loved how chilled Flynn always was around James. Most guys seemed to wind him up but James had the opposite effect – calming him down, smoothing him out.

So what if Dad wouldn't let Flynn stay on the commune. I would just refuse to go too. The whole summer was coming up and, okay, so Flynn was going to have to work long hours and carry on sleeping on people's sofas, but we would be together.

'I guess we can tell other people you're back now,' I said.

Flynn nodded. Then he turned to James and Grace and his face grew uncharacteristically serious.

'Thank you for keeping me a secret before,' he

said to them. 'I don't know what River and I would have done without you.'

Silence fell. In the distance I could hear Grace's nine-year-old twin sisters shrieking with laughter. Across the room, Grace herself was blushing and James looked self-conscious too. No wonder . . . Flynn rarely talked about his feelings or sounded vulnerable, like he had just then. It was a sign of how much James meant to him – and, I supposed, maybe another result of his counselling sessions.

'Well, that's enough mush for one evening.' Flynn leaned across me to fiddle with Grace's laptop. He pressed play on a loud indie track that filled the air with a screaming guitar solo, then announced he needed a pee and left the room.

'I'm gonna go too . . . get some drinks.' Grace drifted to the door. In the past couple of months she'd grown a few centimetres and had lost the slightly waif-like little-girl look she'd had when I met her. I realised with a jolt, as she turned to face me and James, that Grace was now truly beautiful – with her sleek blonde hair and high cheekbones, she looked like a model. She smiled her shy smile at us as she left the room. 'Be good, you two.'

The words hung in the air. The screaming guitar track came to an end. A beat passed in the silence. I looked at James and knew he was thinking about the same moment from the past that I was.

'I told Grace about that evening you were drunk, River,' he said softly.

A wave of shame washed over me. Back in February, when Flynn had been in Ireland, I'd thought for a few nights he might not want me anymore. I'd got drunk at a club and, after fending off one guy whose slug-tongued attempt at kissing me had left me feeling sick, ended up making poor James kiss me on the way home in our taxi. The kiss had lasted about two seconds and meant nothing. We'd agreed we should keep quiet about it and, after a few days of feeling insanely guilty, I had actually put the whole episode out of my mind.

'You told Grace?' I couldn't believe it. '*Why?* Was she okay about it?'

James nodded. 'We were out a couple of weeks ago. This guy lunged at her while I was in the bathroom. I came out to find him pinning her against the wall. I was mad at her for a bit, till she explained what happened . . . then I told her how you'd lunged at me that time and how drunk you were and how bad you'd felt . . .'

'Jeez.' My stomach knotted. I had tried hard not to think about that night for such a long time and now the memory was vivid in my head again. I filled up with a terrible, burning humiliation. I couldn't believe how selfish, how thoughtless I had been. 'Was Grace really cool about it?'

'Yeah, she got it . . . she understood it was no big deal. We had a laugh about it, actually,' he said.

I chewed on my lip, still feeling anxious. I wasn't sure I'd have been so understanding. But then Grace had always been more even-tempered than me . . . less prone to seeing things in extreme terms.

James coughed, lowering his voice. 'Er . . . we agreed that Flynn still shouldn't know, though.'

'No,' I said fervently. 'He shouldn't. *Definitely*.' I knew Flynn would never be as easy-going about the whole thing as Grace. Anyway, James had done nothing wrong. The kiss was my fault. And Flynn would find it hard to understand that.

Later, we went over to James's house. His parents were away for the weekend and we were planning to stay up late watching movies. I hadn't talked to Grace about my 'two-second kiss' with James yet. I knew that I would have to say something eventually, but I had no idea what that should be. Anyway, it was way too risky to mention the subject while Flynn might overhear us.

While the others were making drinks, I slipped

outside into the spacious front garden and called Mum. She was predictably mad that I'd just left the house without talking to her about my relationship with Flynn. But, for once, her annoyance didn't trigger off my own.

After all, what could she do? I was starting to see that I had a lot more power than I'd ever realised.

'My relationship with Flynn isn't any of your business, Mum,' I said calmly.

'Well, I want you to come home so we can discuss it,' she said. 'I've had your father here all day banging on about how we have to find "balance" in how we treat you but as far as I'm concerned, if you're going to behave like a child then I'm going to treat you like one. Stone's gone out to a party so we can have a proper chat and—'

'I'm not coming home tonight, Mum,' I interrupted, irritation starting to crawl across my skin. 'I'm staying over at James's. Grace is here and—'

Mum drew in her breath sharply. 'What about Flynn? Is he there?'

'Of course,' I said. 'He's my boyfriend.'

I steeled myself, ready to argue . . . to defend myself and Flynn . . . but to my surprise Mum just sighed.

'Well, be careful,' she said. 'I'll see you in the morning.'

She rang off. I switched off my phone, feeling troubled. I couldn't really work out why. Truth was, I often felt troubled around Mum. We'd got on so well when I was little – everyone always said how alike we looked and I used to love to copy everything she did. But she seemed to get so controlling once I became a teenager.

'Is everything okay, Riv?' Flynn stepped out from the shadowy wall by the front door.

I started. I hadn't known he was there.

Flynn came over and put his arms around my waist. 'Riv?' he said.

'I was just telling Mum I was staying out tonight,' I said.

'I heard.' Flynn grinned, lowering his face so our lips were just millimetres apart.

I kissed him, feeling the familiar shiver flood through my body. For the first time since I'd known him I felt truly grown-up. I was – for once – in control of my life.

I drew back and studied Flynn's face. I loved him so much. We fitted together so well now. In one sense, we always had. But, for the first few months we'd gone out, Flynn had pushed me over having sex and though I'd said no, I'd always felt awkward about it. For ages now, he hadn't brought it up but it was still there, a conversation that went unsaid.

'I'm ready.' The words came out of my mouth before I knew I was going to say them.

Flynn knew what I meant. I could see it in his eyes.

'You sure?' He tilted his head to one side and raised his eyebrows.

'Yes,' I said. 'More sure than anything.'

We went inside. Flynn said something to James and Grace, then took my hand and led me silently up the stairs to the room we'd stayed in before at the top of the house. It looked just the same as it had done then: fresh and clean with its blue matching bedspread and curtains. My heart beat fast as we closed the curtains. Flynn switched on the lamp that stood on the floor in the corner – it cast a soft glow into the room. Then he wandered over to the bed and kicked off his shoes. He lay down and held out his hand for me. His eyes were dark gold, almost amber – like a lion's.

'Are you really sure?' His voice was low.

'Yes.' I bit my lip. 'But I'm scared.'

I lay down beside him and leaned against his chest. His heart was pounding.

'Me too,' he whispered.

I drew back and blinked up at him. 'You?' I said, genuinely shocked. I couldn't see why Flynn should be scared. He was pretty vague about his exact experiences, but he'd slept with at least two other girls and it wasn't as if we hadn't done almost everything else together already. I rolled my eyes, trying to make a joke of it.

'Bloody hell,' I said. 'I thought at least one of us would know what we were doing.'

Flynn laughed. 'I don't mean I'm scared of the sex,' he said. 'I mean . . .' His face reddened a little. 'I mean I'm scared of not being able to make it good enough. For you.'

My throat felt all choked. I couldn't speak. We stood quite still for a few seconds, then Flynn started unbuttoning my top. 'You look great in this,' he said huskily.

He started stroking his hands over my body. Wherever he touched it was like he was setting fire to me – all I could hear was our breathing – quick and uneven. After a while, he stopped and took a condom out of his pocket.

I held my breath.

Of course, in the end, going all the way wasn't the big deal I'd built it up to be. It certainly didn't last as long as I'd expected. Afterwards, we held each other. My mind raced in about twenty directions. It was done. I had done it. And I'd been totally wrong about it. About what it meant. I'd imagined it would give Flynn power over me. But the way it was between the two of us, it was about each of us *giving up* power, about being vulnerable. Being close to each other.

Flynn lifted his head and smiled. His eyes were soft, almost dreamy, as he kissed my nose. 'That was amazing.'

I smiled at him, and then this great swell of emotion surged up from my stomach. This was it. This was *it*. I couldn't be closer to him than I was right now. I didn't want anything to change. Ever. My face crumpled and I burst into tears.

Flynn stared at me in horror. 'No. Oh God, River. I'm sorry. Oh God, I'm so, so sorry if that was rubbish for you. I promise I'll make it better next—'

'Sssh.' I shook my head, pressing my hand against his mouth. 'I'm crying 'cos I'm happy. 'Cos it was wonderful.'

'Really?' Flynn stared at me for a second.

I nodded. Then I sniffed and wiped my face.

Flynn hugged me again. I could almost feel the happiness coming off him in waves. 'Was it really . . . okay?' he said. He raised his eyebrows, trying to look all ironic and sophisticated.

I laughed. 'You just want me to tell you it was wonderful again.'

Flynn leaned over me. His eyes glinted in the dim light from the floor. He ran his hand down my side and leaned closer until his mouth was right over mine. I shivered, wanting him to kiss me so much I couldn't breathe. 'It'll be more wonderful next time,' he murmured. 'I promise.'

7

I went home late the next morning in a daze. I'd switched my phone on as I walked away from James's house, expecting there to be a million messages from Mum and Dad. But there weren't any. I pocketed the mobile and turned onto Crouch End Broadway, wondering what that was about. My head was still full of making love with Flynn – what we'd done last night wasn't so different from how we'd been together before, and yet it seemed to take us to a new level, to something bigger and stronger than we'd shared before.

My house was only fifteen minutes' walk away from James's and it felt good to be strolling along in the sunshine. Above me, the sky was clear – it looked like today was going to be another beautiful day. I sighed with contentment. And then I saw Emmi. She was walking towards me, her eyes focused on her phone. She glanced up. Saw me. A second later and we were right in front of each other. We stopped walking. I gulped, feeling awkward.

Up until Flynn's return in March, Emmi had been my best friend. Smart, pretty and outrageously self-confident, she had taken me and Grace under her wing during our first term at Langton Girls Grammar nearly six years ago. The three of us had been inseparable.

'Hi, River.' Emmi sounded guarded.

Well, her tone wasn't really surprising. The two of us hadn't met up out of school for weeks. I was the one who'd withdrawn, but Emmi hadn't helped. You see, at the start of the year Emmi's boyfriend Alex had accused Flynn of stealing his iPad. But I found out, back in March, that Alex had only pretended the iPad was missing in order to get his parents to claim a better version on the insurance. For reasons which I couldn't now remember, I'd promised never to tell Emmi that I knew.

Like most of the other things I'd ever promised to keep quiet about, this had turned out to be a mistake. It's hard to be best friends with someone when you're keeping such a massive secret from them. Anyway, like I said, Emmi hadn't made it easy to carry on being friends. Even though it was obvious, when the iPad turned up, that Flynn couldn't have stolen it, Emmi still made snide comments about him . . . about how I was better off without him. This was bad enough when Flynn and I were apart but it was doubly hard to take once we were secretly back together.

'Hi, Emmi.' I smiled. 'How are you doing?'

Emmi shrugged. 'Fine.' She looked angry. Was that because I hadn't called her? The truth was that I'd wanted, many times over the past three months, to tell Emmi that Flynn was back from Ireland and that we were seeing each other again but it was just too risky. I couldn't trust that she wouldn't tell Alex and, if Alex found out I was sure he'd try and get Flynn into trouble again. Still, now I'd told Mum and Dad, it didn't really matter who knew.

'It's good to see you, Riv.' Emmi sniffed.

I peered more closely at her. Perhaps she wasn't mad at me after all. She seemed more miserable than cross. Under her expert make-up, her skin, normally smooth and tanned, was blotchy and the whites of her velvety-brown eyes looked pink and sore. Had she been *crying*?

'Are you okay, Em?' I couldn't believe she wasn't. Emmi was always so sure of herself . . . and she led a charmed life. At home her parents spoiled her, at school the teachers loved her and she was universally popular. Alex adored her and, wherever she went, boys fell at her feet. I couldn't imagine what would make her so upset.

Emmi's mouth wobbled. Huge tears welled up in her eyes and her mouth crumpled.

'Oh, Emmi.' I forgot the distance of the past few months and just felt for my friend. I put my arms around her and she sobbed into my shoulder. 'What's the matter?'

Emmi pulled back, sniffing and wiping her eyes. 'Nothing.' A fresh tear trickled down her cheek.

'Emmi?' I raised my eyebrows. 'Come on.'

'Okay.' She sniffed again. 'Me and Alex split . . . he dumped me.'

My mouth fell open. I couldn't imagine why Alex would give Emmi up – she was gorgeous and smart and, I knew for a fact, most of his friends envied him massively for having her as a girlfriend.

'What? *Why?*' I said.

Emmi's cheeks pinked. 'He found me with someone else.'

I stared at her. 'Who?'

'No one you know . . . just a guy I met the other day. It didn't mean anything.' She sighed. 'It didn't mean *anything*. I was just messing about.'

'Did you explain that to Alex?' I said. My mind flashed back to that kiss with James. That had meant nothing. *Less* than nothing.

Emmi nodded. 'Thing is . . .' she hesitated. 'It wasn't the first time it . . . that had happened. Alex said he couldn't trust me anymore.'

'Oh, I see.' I guess that did put a different slant on it. Still, poor Emmi. And poor Alex.

I gazed around. The Broadway was bustling, a busy Monday morning. Everything felt strange . . . me and Flynn sleeping together last night . . . my row with Mum and Dad and them not calling me . . . and now bumping into Emmi and us talking like old friends even though we weren't so close anymore . . .

'Well, don't take this the wrong way, Emmi, but maybe it was meant to be. I mean, if you really liked Alex you wouldn't have kept going off with other people, would you? So . . . so maybe it's not such a bad thing you've broken up . . .'

Emmi's forehead crinkled into a frown. She pushed back her long, wavy brown hair with a typically haughty flick of the hand. 'Of *course* it's not a bad thing. I'm just upset he dumped me . . . you know, before I had a chance to dump him.'

I burst out laughing. That was so typical of Emmi. I felt a wave of affection for her wash over me. Yes, she was abrasive and shallow sometimes, but she was also funny and quick – qualities which, if I was honest, Grace lacked and which I missed.

Emmi laughed too, her face lighting up. Two guys walked past as she did so and they both stared, mesmerised by her pretty face.

'I don't think you'll have any problem finding a new boyfriend,' I said, rolling my eyes.

Emmi giggled. 'Oh, who wants a boyfriend! Say, River, are you going anywhere right now? D'you fancy getting a drink at Melon Head?'

Melon Head was the latest juice bar that had opened up in Crouch End. I hadn't been there yet but I'd heard lots of good reports.

'Sure, I was only going home,' I said, grimacing. 'And anything that puts off having to talk to Mum is a good thing.'

'Really?' Emmi linked arms with me and we strolled down the street to the juice bar. Inside, Melon Head was cool, all chrome and mirrors. I was certain the drinks were going to be expensive. Still, Emmi always had loads of money and, right now, I felt kind of reckless about everything.

'What's up with you and your mum?' Emmi asked.

I took a deep breath.

'Mum found out something,' I said.

Emmi looked up. 'What?'

'It's Flynn. He came back from Ireland a few months ago,' I said, deciding just to come straight out with it. 'He and I have been going back out in secret for a bit. Mum's really angry about it.'

'Oooh.' Emmi's eyes widened. 'Tell me everything.'

So I told her. We ended up chatting for over an hour. I apologised for not telling her about Flynn's return before, hinting that I was worried that if Alex had found out the news might have got back to my parents.

To my surprise Emmi acknowledged this straight away.

'Yeah, he always had such a downer on Flynn. You know, I think it was because he was jealous of him.'

'Jealous?' I said.

'Of how Flynn didn't care what people thought of him, mostly.' Emmi sipped at her juice. 'And the way Flynn seemed to get good marks in everything without ever trying. Alex was nice but not that good at school stuff, you know? His dad was always making comparisons with his older brothers. Alex let it get to him.'

'I had no idea,' I said.

Emmi set down her glass.

'I'm sorry I was always so rude about Flynn too,' she said awkwardly. 'I guess maybe I was a bit jealous myself – not of him personally, but of how loved-up the two of you were . . . are . . .' She smiled, her eyes softening.

I stared at her. Never in a million years had I imagined that Emmi would envy me and Flynn our relationship. She always seemed so happy with her own life. For the first time, it struck me how hard it is ever to really understand another person. The thought made me shiver. Still, Flynn and I understood each other, didn't we? That was part of what made our relationship so special.

'Anyway . . .' Emmi sipped at her juice again. 'It's great you're back together, Riv. I'm really pleased for you.'

'Thanks.' I squeezed her hand.

We chatted on. It was fun. I even promised Emmi I'd go round to her place at the weekend to hang out – and that I'd persuade Flynn to come to our school's end-of-year party the following week. He'd already said he didn't want to go to his own prom but maybe he wouldn't mind coming to mine with me. I hadn't given it much thought before but it would be fun, especially if I was never going back to that school.

That thought reminded me of Mum and Dad and our earlier argument over my moving to the commune. Suddenly I felt sure that I wanted to live there; it had been great to see Emmi – and I would definitely miss her and Grace – but I was ready for a fresh start. Anyway, the commune wasn't a million miles away. I'd still be able to see my London friends on a regular basis.

I said goodbye to Emmi and set off for home. Mum would probably be in and alone when I got there. I would tackle her again, straight away, pointing out all the reasons why a fresh start at a new sixth form college would be good for me before bringing Flynn into the argument.

It was almost one o'clock when I fitted my key into the front door. I could hear voices coming from the kitchen. Mum and Stone were talking . . . *damn*, so she wasn't alone. Wait, was that *Dad* weighing in too?

I scurried across the hall. The three of them were sitting around the kitchen table eating lunch – a couple of quiches and a bowl of salad stood in the middle of the table. A bottle of wine was open too.

What was going on? I couldn't remember the last time Mum and Dad had been together for a family meal.

The three of them looked up as I walked in. Dad smiled but Mum pursed her lips.

'Ah, the wanderer returns,' she said sharply.

'Hi, sis,' Stone said.

I looked at him in surprise. Stone spent most of his time skulking about the house, holed up in his room. I remember Mum saying he was going to a party last night. I peered more closely. Was that a love bite on his neck? I suppressed a giggle. My spotty, lanky, fourteen-year-old brother was getting interest from girls. Could this day get any weirder?

'What's going on?' I said.

Mum put down her knife and fork. They clattered against her plate. 'I'm fed up with you treating this house like a hotel, River.'

I opened my mouth to protest but Mum held up her hand. 'Let's not argue about it,' she said. 'Your dad stayed last night so he could be here when you got back, so we could talk.'

My mouth fell open. Dad had stayed at our house?

'We spoke for a long time about what's best for you,' Mum went on. 'You've made it clear that you can't wait to get away from here and go and live on the commune – not just for the summer, but permanently.'

She paused. I flushed with embarrassment. The way Mum was speaking, all cold and hard, made it sound like I wanted to go away from home to punish her.

'It's not about getting away from *you*, Mum,' I said. 'And you suggested me moving to the commune yourself a few months ago.'

'I know,' Mum said. She pursed her lips. 'But that was only if you refused to stop seeing Flynn—'

'Which I do.'

'I know.'

We stared at each other. I could sense Dad and Stone watching us. A lump formed in my throat. I hated Mum being so angry with me. Tears welled in my eyes. Mum shook her head, then she sighed. 'I don't want you to leave, River, but I appreciate that you're nearly seventeen and old enough to start making some of your own decisions.'

I glanced at Dad. He nodded.

'We've checked out the sixth form college you're so set on transferring to,' Mum went on.

'Norton Napier?'

Mum nodded. 'Their website is very impressive and so are their results. I called them this morning and, provided you meet the entry criteria with your GCSEs, they say they'll have a place for you.'

'Really?'

'The three of us should visit this week, just to be sure,' Dad added. 'But if you still want to go there after the visit that's fine with Mum and me.'

My heart thumped with excitement. And apprehension. This was *epic*. Mum was actually agreeing to me going to live with Dad. I could hardly believe it.

'And I'm having your room here.' Stone grinned, getting up from the table and heading for the door.

'What?' For a second I wanted to protest. After all, suppose I wanted to come back at some point? Still, who was to say I wouldn't be just as happy in a new place? Or that Stone himself wouldn't have left home by the time college was over. After all, he was only two years younger than me.

'It's only fair, River,' Dad said softly as Stone left the room. 'If you're sure this is really what you want.'

'It is, I'm *so* ready to leave Langton.' As I said the words, my life at school flashed before my eyes. I'd been at Langton since I was eleven and I knew every nook and cranny of the place. Life there was easy. Comfortable.

Which was part of the problem. It was *too* comfortable. I was ready for adventure, for a new life, for a new life with Flynn.

Flynn.

'What about . . . the other thing?' I asked.

Mum and Dad exchanged glances.

Dad cleared his throat. 'You mean Flynn?'

I nodded, my throat suddenly dry.

'I don't want you seeing him,' Mum said, folding her arms. 'I certainly don't want him living there with you but your father seems to think Flynn deserves a second chance . . .' She sniffed.

'Everyone deserves a second chance,' Dad said.

He turned to me. 'River, I've thought very carefully about Flynn joining the commune. I've already talked to Gemma but I need to discuss it with everyone else who lives there. That's how we make decisions there, everyone together.'

'But they won't mind,' I said eagerly. 'They'll understand it's a way of helping him, won't they?'

'I think so,' Dad acknowledged. 'Everyone's certainly very aware that right now Flynn doesn't have a proper home in London *and* that he's working hard and attending counselling sessions to deal with his anger. The commune ethos is all about shared support and when you take into account Flynn's age and his background and all the efforts he's making to turn things around for himself, well, it's impressive.' He hesitated. 'But Flynn's got to jump through some hoops too.'

'What hoops?'

'Flynn's made a good start with the counselling but he still has a lot to do to prove himself, so we want him to continue seeing someone – there are several options at the place where Gemma works, so—'

'I'm sure that will be fine,' I interrupted. After all, hadn't Flynn spoken positively about the therapy he was having? I couldn't imagine he would object to continuing it once he was living at the commune.

'Good,' Dad said. 'So ... clearly Flynn's trying hard to get things right and he obviously cares about you very much.'

'Oh, he does,' I said, clasping my hands together. 'He *does*, Dad. And I *really* care about him.'

Mum snorted. From outside in the hall Stone made puking noises.

I ignored them both. 'So are you saying Flynn can stay too?'

'Whoa, River.' Dad took my hands. 'What we're saying is this: as soon as your school term officially ends, you move into the commune. Alone. You'll be expected to take on proper chores and Flynn can visit at weekends, when he will also have responsibilities.'

'He won't mind that,' I said, my excitement building. 'But what about the sixth form college? What about when term starts?'

'Well, Flynn needs to make contact with them directly, but there should be no problem. He easily has the grades to get in and the college definitely has places.'

'So you're saying ... ?'

Dad threw another look at Mum. She was sitting very still in her chair, her eyes on the plate in front of her. Dad turned back to me.

'I'm saying that if Flynn does everything that's

asked of him then he can move in permanently for the start of school in September. Separate rooms, though. Flynn will have to stay on the sofa until we can sort something out for him.'

'Oh, Dad!' I flung my arms around him, happiness overwhelming me. 'Thank you!'

I could hear a chair scraping across the kitchen floor. Out of the corner of my eye I could see Mum walking away, out of the room. Dad hugged me back.

'Remember, Flynn will have to keep seeing a counsellor,' he said. 'That's an important condition. Gemma was suggesting group counselling might be helpful and we expect Flynn to be open to that process, just as—'

'Oh, he will be.' I nestled in close against Dad's chest, breathing in his safe, solid, earthy smell.

Dad kissed the top of my head. 'It'll be so wonderful having you live with us, darling,' he said. 'Just don't stop being my little girl . . . not quite yet.'

8

I called Flynn straight away and told him Dad had agreed to us both moving into the commune. He couldn't believe it. We met in the park a few hours later; it was still light, a warm, sunny evening. We lay stretched out on the grass and Flynn wound my hair around his fingers as I explained the conditions Dad had laid down. I was a little worried that he might baulk at the idea of being told what to do but, instead, a slow smile spread over his face.

'So we'll be able to stay together? Make that store-room into a proper bedroom?'

'Dad doesn't want us to sleep together, though,' I reminded him. 'You've got to stay on the sofa, at least at first.'

Flynn waved this away. 'We'll sort that,' he said. 'We'll be living together. *And* going to the same school. A proper sixth form college just around the corner.'

'That's right.'

'And all I'll have to do in return is go to group therapy and spend eighteen hours a week or whatever working on the commune?' he asked. 'Mending fences or taking a turn washing up . . . that sort of thing?'

'Yes, but . . .' I frowned. I couldn't exactly put my finger on what it was, but there was surely something missing from Flynn's summary. Commune living wasn't just about doing chores in return for a free room. It was about joining in, being part of something bigger than an individual life.

'You'll still have to get on with everyone . . . no fights or anything,' I said. 'And you haven't seen the sixth form college yet. Or Gemma's place where they do the group counselling.'

Flynn sat up, waving his hand dismissively again. 'None of that will be a problem. And I've totally worked out the therapy thing now.'

'What do you mean?' I said. Across the park a group of little boys were arguing over a football. One of them picked up the ball and ran off to the swings. The others chased after him.

Flynn shrugged. 'What they want to hear is how you're taking responsibility for your anger, not blaming other people for how you feel.'

'Oh.' I wasn't sure what to say. Flynn hadn't

talked much about his counselling sessions. I had no idea how they worked. 'So . . . do you often still get the urge to hit people?' I asked with a smile, trying to make my question sound light and casual.

Flynn grinned. 'Sometimes, but I don't do it, that's the point.'

The little boys with the football ran back onto the grass behind Flynn but I kept my focus on him.

'What d'you mean?' I asked. 'What stops you?'

'I've got . . . what do they call them? Yeah, *strategies*.' Flynn said the word with heavy emphasis. 'I've got strategies for dealing with it when I lose my temper. You know, like focusing on something else. It's cool, Riv. Don't worry.'

I pressed my hands into the grass. The earth was dry against my palms. 'So you're pleased?' I said.

'I'm d-e-lirious with d-e-light,' Flynn said, his voice growling over the words. Then he leaned right over me. 'Let me show you how much.'

Term officially ended a couple of weeks later. By that point I had visited Norton Napier with Mum – and been really impressed by the college. The syllabuses they followed here for History and English looked much more interesting than the courses I would have had to take at Langton. I could even do Psychology, which wasn't on offer at all at my old school. Flynn had also visited, though he had gone separately and on his own. When we talked afterwards he sounded just as excited as I was about the college, though for a different reason. 'The important thing is that they'll take us both, Riv,' he said. 'I'll get my As wherever we are.'

From anyone else it might have sounded arrogant but Flynn was just stating facts. He was smart and focused and he'd *always* had great grades.

The last few days of school passed in a blur. Flynn came with me to the Langton end-of-year party and we had a great time. Emmi made an effort to be really friendly with Flynn who, in turn, was much nicer to her than he used to be. I guess it helped that she was no longer going out with Alex.

Alex himself wasn't at the prom, of course, but James came along with Grace and he and Flynn had a blast. They dressed in suits (Flynn borrowed his from James's brother) and heckled when our year captain, Daisy Walker, whom they both knew from *Romeo and Juliet*, was doing her rather formal 'thank-you' speech to everyone who had helped organise the party.

Lots of girls threw Flynn admiring glances as we passed. I saw him notice these – and the girls' long legs and short skirts – but he still spent almost the entire evening by my side, his arm around my shoulder. I, for once, felt good about how I looked. I was wearing a silvery, backless dress of Emmi's that clung to my hips then floated prettily over my thighs. Both she and Grace had said I looked amazing in it and, from the look on Flynn's face when he saw me, I was hoping they were right.

It was late and the others were all on the dance floor when I slipped outside for some air. I was just standing, leaning against the wall by the fire door, when I heard footsteps behind me and turned to see Grace coming out too. She was in a light blue dress, much shorter than she would normally wear, and a pair of Emmi's killer heels. Her pale cheeks were flushed and her blonde hair tousled.

She saw me and groaned. 'These shoes are killing me,' she said, leaning against the wall to take them off.

As she straightened up, she shook her hair off her face. Once again, I was struck by how pretty she had become in the past year or so.

'You look amazing,' I said.

She rolled her eyes but I could tell she was pleased. I suddenly remembered what James had told me the other day, that Grace knew about our stupid kiss in the back of that taxi. I'd been avoiding talking to her about it but now I knew I had to say something.

'Grace, there's something I need to talk to you about,' I started, my heart suddenly thumping.

She met my gaze. For a moment she looked confused, then her expression clouded slightly.

'No,' she said quietly. 'You really don't need to say anything.'

The space between us grew tense. Music blared out from inside the hall, people talking and laughing. Traffic hummed in the distance.

'I'm just so sorry, Grace.' I could feel my face burning red. 'I was *really* drunk, Grace. I didn't even want to . . . I just—'

'I know.' Grace looked down at her dress, her face flushed. 'James told me: you were unhappy about Flynn and going on about this guy – Slug Tongue – who'd kissed you and . . . and you said that you wanted him to take away the feel of it or something . . .'

I nodded, shame overwhelming me. 'That's right. Oh, Grace . . .' I stopped. I couldn't think what to say. I tried to imagine how I'd feel if she'd kissed Flynn. It was impossible. There was no way Flynn would have let it happen. Not unless he'd wanted it to. Which wasn't how it had been with James.

'It wasn't James's fault, Grace. You have to believe that. I was out of my head with drink and missing Flynn and thinking he didn't love me and . . . and I just . . . it just happened. It lasted about one nano-second, *nothing*, then I realised what I was doing and . . . I *hated* myself for losing control like that.' Tears welled up at the terrible memory.

'It's okay, River.' Grace looked up at me. Her eyes were sad but I could see no anger in her expression. 'James only told me because he felt bad about us having secrets from each other. He said it meant nothing. He said he told you not to say anything to me because it would just upset me.' She sighed miserably. 'But I'd rather know the truth.'

My chest tightened. 'Oh, Grace, thank you . . . I'm still so, so sorry.' I swallowed down the lump in my throat, hating myself for hurting her.

'I know you are.' She smiled again, this time more brightly. 'Let's go back inside. Maybe if you can't stop feeling guilty I should go and have sex with Flynn to even things up.' She laughed.

I stared at her. I'd never heard Grace say anything that outrageous before.

'Your face!' Grace laughed. 'What, you think it's only you and Emmi who can say stuff like that?' She took my hand. 'Come on, Riv, forget it, it's over. Let's go and have some fun.'

We walked back into the hall. Flynn was dancing in a big, mixed group. I stood for a moment, watching him move. He danced as well as he did everything, his movements smooth yet powerful. Again, I noticed several girls from my year eyeing him up. One – a blonde with long, slim legs from one of the parallel classes – leaned up to say something to him. Flynn pushed his hair off his face and bent closer to listen to her. A sliver of jealousy lodged itself in my stomach. I raced over, only slowing to a saunter as I approached the dance floor. Flynn must have felt me looking. He glanced up from the blonde girl, saw me and smiled.

He looked so gorgeous and so happy to see me that I forgot about being jealous. The girl beside him melted away as I rushed over and hugged him hard.

He hugged me back and then we kissed. Right there, right then, a big, long, sexy kiss while around us the dancers whirled and the music soared.

School ended the next day and, the day after that, Dad came to collect me and all my stuff. I'd packed a couple of suitcases with my clothes and the little ornaments and make-up stuff I had on my side table plus a few old toys I didn't want to leave behind.

My head was still full of how emotional my final day at Langton had been – everyone hugging and weeping, signing each other's school shirts and promising never to lose touch if we lived to be a hundred.

For a few minutes, as I walked home that day, I felt sad to be leaving. I would miss Langton, especially all my friends there. Yet I knew it was time for me to move on. I would still see Emmi and Grace and, of course, I would make new friends at the sixth form college.

Most importantly of all, I would be with Flynn.

It was weird saying goodbye to Mum. Neither of us cried but I think both of us felt like it. I thought it would be liberating leaving the house and my old life but, as we drove away, I felt strange, like my old life was leaving *me*. I took a few deep breaths. Soon I would have a new room. Dad said he had already taken most of the junk out of the storeroom and had promised to help me and Flynn decorate it this weekend. Stone wasn't going to come up this week – he was still at school – and Dad said they'd need the living room to put the furniture from the storeroom in while we painted.

We picked Flynn up on the way. He had changed his shifts so that he could have weekends free to spend at the commune. We sat on the back seat, holding hands all the way. Flynn was quieter than on his last visit, but keen to get started on decorating the storeroom. Dad ran through our chores for the weekend. Washing up after the evening meal tonight, then working on the storeroom on Saturday. On Sunday morning Flynn was scheduled to work outside on the south field, while I was down to help prepare Sunday lunch in the kitchen.

'Do we have to eat *every* meal with everyone else?' Flynn asked.

'Well, mostly, yes,' Dad said, sounding puzzled. 'That's kind of the point of living in the commune. I thought you understood how it worked.'

'We do, Dad.' I grinned at Flynn. 'It's just a bit boring for us, you know, with everyone else being so old.'

'Well, Leo's here now,' Dad said. 'He'll be company for you.'

'Who's Leo?' That was Flynn.

'Was he the one visiting with his dad the other day?' I asked.

'That's right,' Dad said, taking the turn signposted for Norton.

'I met him for about five minutes,' I explained to Flynn. 'He was nice, though maybe a bit odd. His mum died last year, he told me, and his dad isn't handling it all that well and he's my age, starting at the sixth form college in September like we are.'

Flynn raised his eyebrows. 'You found out a lot in just five minutes,' he said. His voice was carefully light, but I could hear the slight edge to it.

'Like I said, Leo's kind of odd. Anyway, don't worry, he's not my type.'

Flynn poked me in the arm. 'Better not be,' he said with a grin.

Ros and Gemma were waiting outside when we arrived at the commune. We said hello then rushed upstairs to dump our bags. The storeroom looked far bigger than usual. Dad had cleared out the camp bed and all the planks of wood and cardboard boxes and moved in a small double bed, a wooden chest of drawers with paint peeling from its sides and a hanging rail that ran along the small wall to the door. A new daisy-chain print curtain fluttered at the window. It reminded me of one I'd had when I was little.

'Is it okay?' Dad asked anxiously. 'I know it needs a lick of paint, but—'

'It's perfect, Dad,' I breathed.

'It's awesome,' Flynn added.

'You do understand you'll just be using the room to store your clothes, don't you, Flynn?' Dad gave him a stern look.

A shadow passed over Flynn's face. I took his

hand quickly, then turned to Dad and smiled. 'Course he does.'

'Okay,' Dad said. 'Well, dinner in ten. See you downstairs in a minute.' He left the rooms.

Flynn and I looked at each other.

'I'm not staying outside all night on the sofa, whatever he says,' Flynn said.

'I know.' I grinned. 'Just make sure Dad doesn't see you sneaking about.'

Flynn shrugged.

'Hey,' I said, taking his hand. 'As far as I'm concerned, this is *our room*.'

The shadow lifted from Flynn's face. He tugged me towards the bed and we lay down. I breathed in the scent from the white duvet cover: fresh and clean and comforting.

Flynn put his arms round me. 'River?' he whispered. 'Welcome home.'

We spent the whole of the next day working hard on the bedroom. Flynn and Dad sanded the floor first thing, while I took the chest of drawers outside and gave it a lick of fresh blue paint. Feeling suddenly artistic, I dabbed a row of white daisies down the sides, then left the whole thing to dry.

Once the floor was sanded, Flynn and I covered the walls with white emulsion, then Dad came back in to help us varnish the floorboards. It wasn't a massive room but by the time we stopped at nine that evening, the three of us had been working flat out for nearly twelve hours and were utterly exhausted. Flynn insisted on going back up after dinner – once the floor varnish had dried – and putting eggshell paint on the windowsill and frame.

'He works hard, I'll give him that,' Dad said as we sipped at a cup of tea outside, waiting for Flynn to finish.

That night I slept on the bed in the middle of the room with the windows wide open against the smell of the paint. Flynn, as agreed, started out on the living room sofa but snuck into my bed once Dad and Gemma had closed their door. He was still there, his hair half over his face, when I woke up. I gazed down at him. This didn't feel real. I couldn't believe we were here together – that this was my new home. After a few minutes, I woke Flynn so that he could go back to the sofa before Dad got up. He grumbled a bit but went readily enough. Neither of us wanted a big row at this point, though I could see the situation as it was couldn't last forever.

Flynn and I did our work the following day, then Flynn left to go back to North London and his various jobs. I spent the rest of the week doing my chores and working on our room. I missed Flynn, of course

– and it was weird not being able just to pop out and see Emmi and Grace, like I'd used to, but I didn't miss living with Mum or Stone and, anyway, I had the thought of next weekend and Flynn's return to keep me going.

As soon as he arrived the following Friday evening, I took his hand.

'Come up and see what I've done,' I said.

'Dinner in an hour,' Gemma smiled, as we rushed through the kitchen.

I'd worked hard on our room since he'd been gone and was proud of the result. The floor gleamed and the walls sparkled and all the little ornaments and photos I'd set out made the place seem really cosy.

Flynn wandered from the bed to the chest of drawers, lingering over the array of bottles and bowls that sat on its surface.

'What do you think?' I asked. 'Does it feel like home?'

He turned to me and nodded. 'It's brilliant, River.' He held up a chain from one of the bowls. It was broken at the catch, but the tiny blue 'R' still dangled from one end.

'I've never seen you wearing this,' he said.

I stared at the necklace. 'Grace gave it to me,' I said. 'The first birthday I had after starting at Langton and meeting her and Emmi. The catch broke ages ago. I forgot I had it until I was going through my stuff from Mum's.'

I held up my wrist, from which the silver heart Flynn had given me dangled on its slim bracelet. 'To be honest, I forgot I had any other jewellery apart from this.'

Flynn smiled. 'I'll mend the necklace for you, if you like?'

'Thanks.' I looked around the room again. It felt so grown-up, so romantic to have a place of our own. 'So you really like what I've done in here?'

'It's amazing, Riv,' Flynn said, pocketing the broken chain. 'Home.'

Leo and his dad were at our evening meal that night. Flynn hadn't really spoken to Leo last weekend but this time he took the trouble to chat, asking him if he was looking forward to starting at Norton Napier in September, and whether or not he played football. Leo didn't play. In fact, he seemed very subdued throughout the meal and answered Flynn mostly in monosyllables.

'Leo's really weird, isn't he?' Flynn said later, when we were up in our room. 'He didn't seem to want to speak to me.'

I sighed, remembering how quickly Leo had spilled all that stuff to me, about his mum dying and his dad freaking out.

'Maybe you frightened him,' I suggested with a smile.

'Maybe he's gay and finds me so devastatingly attractive that he doesn't know *what* to say to me,' Flynn said with a grin.

I rolled my eyes at him but the truth was that this possibility had occurred to me too. It might explain why Leo had been so awkward around Flynn.

I went back to London that week, to see Mum. Not that she and I really talked anymore. She'd already let Stone take my bedroom – it was unrecognisable, the walls covered with posters of indie bands and girls in bikinis. I spent my second evening out with Emmi and Grace. Emmi was full of questions about life on the commune.

'How do you cope, River?' she asked, wide-eyed. 'All that mud and the wild animals and the cold water.'

I rolled my eyes. 'There isn't any mud in the middle of summer and, for your information, hens aren't wild animals and the water is perfectly hot – at least it is in the mornings and evenings.'

Emmi was going to France for a month – she was clearly totally over Alex already and massively excited about all the gorgeous French boys she was hoping to meet.

'But I'll come and visit when I'm back, River,' she grinned. 'Check out the commune. Plus your Leo sounds sweet.' She winked at Grace, who blushed.

'He's not "my Leo".' I rolled my eyes. 'And I'm not letting you anywhere near him.'

The thought of predatory Emmi trying to get her claws into poor, anxious, possibly gay Leo was more than I could stand.

Emmi raised her eyebrows. 'You sound possessive, River.'

'No, I'm not,' I protested. 'It is possible to get on with a boy without wanting to do it with them, you know.'

Emmi laughed.

'James and I are definitely going to come for a visit before the holidays finish,' Grace said. 'My dad's got a tent we could use. It'll be so cool sleeping out of doors.'

'Awesome,' I said, though I didn't really see the attraction of spending the night outdoors myself, not when there was a nice soft mattress in our room.

Our room.

Emmi narrowed her eyes as if she'd seen my thoughts. 'I'm sure it feels great now but once you're together full time, you won't ever be able to get away. There'll be nowhere to hide out when you've got a zit or had an argument or when your period's making you feel like rubbish.'

'Flynn doesn't care about those things,' I said, defiantly. But inside I couldn't help but feel a bit anxious. Emmi had a point, after all. What was it going to be like once Flynn was permanently living on the commune?

9

As it turned out, it was bliss.

Mostly.

Certainly, over the summer it was perfect. Once Flynn arrived for the weekend, we spent all our time together. At first Dad insisted he waited until Friday evening before arriving and left before dinner on Sunday night but pretty soon Flynn was coming up on Friday mornings and, after three or four weeks, he was arriving on Thursday afternoons and not leaving again until Monday lunchtime.

We settled easily into a routine: sleeping late, then grabbing some toast for breakfast before starting our chores. Flynn always snuck into my room once Dad and Gemma had gone to bed. They must have known – as they had to pass the sofa on the way to our shared bathroom – but neither of them ever said anything and Flynn was always back on the sofa before morning.

On Fridays and Saturdays we had to sweep and clean the downstairs rooms and communal toilets then we went outside, where our jobs varied each week, though often involved the vegetable patch and the hens. On Sundays we usually joined everyone else tending to the sheep or working in the apple orchard – the organic apples that we would harvest in September were one of the commune's main sources of income. On Sunday nights Flynn and I always helped whoever was in charge of that evening's meal. This meant peeling potatoes if it was the nerdy IT guy, experimenting with spices if it was Gemma or John and giggling over bizarre recipes if Ros was in charge.

We only had to work two or three hours each day and, after our chores were done, we were free. The first half of August was blisteringly hot and sometimes we just sat outside in the long grass near the hen house, reading in the shade all afternoon. I pored over novels – romantic ones, mostly. Nothing heavy. Flynn studied what he needed to for his A levels. Moving to the sixth form college meant he had to change exam syllabuses and therefore was behind on some of his reading, but Flynn was unfazed about catching up. I'd always known he worked hard but, seeing him that summer, I realised I'd never met anyone so disciplined.

Flynn was determined to get into law school and had already looked into the best courses around the country. Whenever he talked about it my stomach tightened into a knot. I couldn't bear the thought of him going away – even though it would be over a year from now – and leaving me behind.

Some days we went out, into the countryside near the commune. We'd wander around woods and fields, hand in hand, talking about stories and music that we liked. We often strolled to the stream that ran through the woods to paddle in the sparkling, shallow water. It was always cold, yet blissful on our hot, tired feet. We'd make out under the trees, then walk some more, finally stopping when we got hungry to eat the snacks and sandwiches we'd brought from the commune.

James and Grace visited a couple of times, camping out in their tent as promised. We hardly saw anyone else. We hardly talked to anyone else. Both of us grew tanned and relaxed, while Flynn was happier than I'd ever seen him. He never shirked his chores or complained about having to do them. He ran every day, usually in the early evening when the sun was past its strongest. And I knew he worked out and shadow-boxed too, though he never let me watch.

He said that he often missed his mum – he emailed her regularly and spoke to her on the phone every week – and that he sometimes missed the gym and his mates there, too, but that being with me more than made up for it.

And me?

I was happier than I'd ever been too. I thought I'd been in love with Flynn before, but this was different. After weeks of spending so much time together, you'd think we'd get bored of each other but we just seemed to keep falling deeper and deeper in love. At night, when Flynn crept into my bed, he would hold me in his arms and whisper how much he loved me.

Not everything was perfect. I knew Dad fretted about the amount of time we spent together. I overheard Gemma reassuring him one day that school would start again in a few weeks and that our lives would open out again.

And then there was Leo. We often saw him in the distance, wandering about on his own. Several times I suggested we include him on our walks, but Flynn always refused.

'He's too weird,' he'd say, wrinkling his nose. Then he'd grin. 'Anyway, I can't share you, Riv.'

It was funny, the way he said it. And flattering, too.

But sometimes, just sometimes, I felt a bit suffocated. Flynn was always an intense person – and to be the object of all his intensity was like standing in the glare of the sun. Warm and beautiful – but sometimes overwhelming.

The weather grew cooler during the last week of August. I got my GCSE results – I'd done well in everything except French and Science, getting mostly As and Bs, with A*s in English and Drama. Flynn had, predictably, got the highest grades possible in all of his AS levels, despite having had to fight to take them in between all his jobs. Now we had our results, our places at Norton Napier were finally confirmed and it felt, suddenly, as if the summer was almost over.

It was time for Dad to let Flynn move in. I was certain that he would. After all, Flynn had done everything Dad had asked of him and more, but as we stood together on the last Saturday in August, waiting to hear what Dad said, I couldn't help but feel anxious.

I needn't have worried. Dad gave us both a smile and said that Flynn had really impressed him over the summer and was free to move in properly whenever he wanted. No one mentioned the issue of Flynn and me sleeping together but after Dad had gone off to water the vegetable patch, Flynn insisted that when he finally brought all his stuff over he was going to stop even pretending to use the sofa.

I was nervous about Dad's reaction so I had a word with Gemma. She promised to talk to Dad about it and, much to my relief, Dad came to me the next day and said that Flynn and me officially sleeping together was fine, so long as I didn't feel under pressure to do so.

'I don't, Dad,' I said, giving him a hug. 'It's really what I want.'

'Okay,' he said, still looking a bit concerned. 'And you're definitely, you know, being safe . . . taking precautions?'

'Yes,' I said, blushing.

'Then I guess that's okay then.' Dad sighed. 'I mean, I'm not wild about it but . . .'

He tailed off and I made some excuse to scuttle away, relieved that the whole business had been resolved at last.

Flynn moved in the following weekend and, for the next fortnight, we were totally inseparable. In fact, the only times we were apart for more than an hour during that period were on the Wednesday evenings when Flynn went for his counselling sessions. He'd had an assessment at the centre earlier in the summer and they'd recommended anger management group therapy. I'd hoped Gemma would run the sessions but she explained that she wasn't a youth specialist.

'Anyway, it wouldn't be right because I already know Flynn,' she said, as we discussed the situation in the kitchen, her rings clinking against her mug of tea. 'It would be too complicated for me to facilitate his sessions. But Sally Dunsford specialises in anger management *and* young people. She'll be perfect.'

I still had no idea what therapy of any kind involved – Flynn hadn't ever talked properly about the counsellor he'd seen in London – but I was sure that the new sessions would continue to help. After all, Flynn was transformed from the person he'd been at the start of the year. He was always respectful with Dad, friendly with Ros and Gemma and polite to everyone else who lived on the commune.

In fact, he hadn't lost his temper for months.

Of course, he had had absolutely nothing to provoke him since we'd moved in together, but I was sure the counselling had made a massive difference too.

Leo sought me out that first Wednesday when Flynn was away, appearing at my side within minutes of Flynn leaving the commune. When I turned and saw him in the kitchen my heart sank. Leo had been so awkward over the summer whenever Flynn and I tried to talk to him. However, as soon as we started chatting, I relaxed. Leo was more fun than I'd expected – all open and enthusiastic about the music he loved. He stuck by my side for the whole hour and a half Flynn was gone, only slinking away out of sight when we heard Flynn's footsteps in the hall.

Leo came and found me again during Flynn's second Wednesday evening counselling session. This time we talked about sixth form college. Our start date was just around the corner and I asked Leo if he felt nervous. He confessed that he did. I'd been feeling a bit anxious about it myself and it was good to know I'd have Leo to turn up with on that first day. Of course, Flynn would be there too, but he was a year older and therefore taking different classes with entirely different people.

Once I'd brought up the subject, Leo chattered away. It turned out that rather than pretend college wasn't happening, which was what I'd done all summer, Leo had read up on our courses. He was studying English, Economics, Spanish and French. I was down to do English, History, Politics and Psychology, so most of our conversations were about the books we were going to be studying for our one shared subject: English Lit.

'I'm glad we're doing Shelley,' Leo said. 'His stuff's amazing. Listen.' He reached for one of the books on the kitchen table and skimmed through the pages. *'True Love in this differs from gold and clay, That to divide is not to take away.'* He looked up at me, this strange, sad expression on his face. 'Isn't that beautiful?'

I nodded. My early impression that Leo was a bit odd, created during our first meeting and borne out through his behaviour over the summer, had only been reinforced during our two long conversations. It wasn't so much the fact that he passionately loved poetry (though admitting to it as freely as he did was certainly unusual) as the intense way he talked about specific poems. In fact, it was the intense way he talked about *everything*. 'There's a bit here that made me think of you.' Leo's pale cheeks blushed as he focused on the page. '. . . *smiling they love and call life pleasure . . .'*

I looked away. It had just occurred to me that Leo might have a bit of a crush on me and the thought left me feeling self-conscious and uncomfortable.

'I think I'll go and find Dad,' I said, standing up and pushing my chair away. 'Before Flynn gets—'

'River?'

I turned back. Leo's eyes were bright against the red of his face.

I frowned. His whole body had tensed. 'What is it?' I asked.

'I think I might be gay,' Leo blurted out.

My eyes widened. So Flynn's hunch had been more or less right after all. I sat down again and stared at Leo. So much for me thinking he might fancy me.

He blinked nervously. 'I don't know for sure, but I think maybe . . .' He tailed off, looking embarrassed.

'Oh.' I had no idea what to say. I wanted to find some way of expressing how I felt, but 'There's nothing wrong with being gay' sounded really patronising, as did telling him that I was really touched he'd confided in me. Anyway, I was more thrown than touched. I hardly knew the guy, yet here he was telling me his deepest secrets.

'Have you ever—' I stopped, my question about whether he'd ever fancied a guy suddenly seemed way too personal. Anyway, suppose Leo liked Flynn, as Flynn had once joked? I felt my face reddening. That would certainly explain why Leo seemed so intimidated by Flynn – and why he steered clear of us as a couple. 'Er, have you talked to your dad about it?' I finally stammered.

Leo raised his eyes. 'You're kidding, right? Dad'd just tell me it was a phase. Anyway, I doubt if he could tear himself away from Ros long enough to listen to me.'

I nodded. Even being completely wrapped up in Flynn as I was, I'd noticed how Leo's dad and Ros had started sitting next to each other every evening at dinner, and laughing hard at everything the other one said.

'Sorry, River, you don't want to hear all this.' Leo put his head in his hands. 'I just don't have anyone else to talk to.'

He stared down at the rough wooden table. Poor guy. Now that I knew he wasn't interested in me I realised all his intense, shiny-eyed looks must be because he felt confused and lonely. I reached out my hand and squeezed his arm.

'You can talk to me anytime you like,' I smiled.

Leo looked up. 'You won't tell anyone, will you?' he said. 'Not even Flynn?'

My two-second kiss with James jumped, unbidden, into my thoughts. I pushed it away. If I wasn't going to tell Flynn about that, there was definitely no need for me to tell him about Leo's worries over his sexuality. After all, it really wasn't any of Flynn's business.

'I won't tell anyone.' I squeezed his arm again. 'I promise.'

The slam of the front door echoed along the corridor towards us. I took my hand off Leo's arm and, a few seconds later, Gemma and Flynn walked into the kitchen.

10

Flynn glanced at me, then at Leo. He scowled. My heart sank. I could tell he was in a bad mood. He'd said his first group therapy session last week had been a bit boring, just a lot of introductions, but nothing that he couldn't handle. He'd seemed quite cheerful in fact.

Tonight was different. He slouched over to the kitchen table and slumped into the chair next to Leo, his long legs sprawled out beside the table. Leo looked away. It was funny seeing them side by side: Flynn radiating his sour mood; dark and troubled and powerful. Leo, like a shadow beside him, blond and pale in comparison, a slighter person, a smaller presence.

'Are you okay?' I asked.

Flynn said nothing. Gemma wandered over to the stove and put the kettle on. I headed to the fridge to get the milk, wondering what the matter was. Leo and I both preferred ordinary tea to Gemma's peppermint. Flynn rarely drank anything except black coffee. I opened the fridge door. Ros's row of beer bottles stared back at me from the top shelf. For a second I considered taking one. I knew Ros wouldn't mind. And Flynn was never bothered about me drinking either, so long as I didn't get drunk. But maybe not tonight. Maybe, right now, if I could just get Flynn to open up in front of Leo, perhaps the three of us could start to be friends.

Closing the fridge door, I placed the milk beside Gemma, hoping she'd make some sign to indicate what had happened tonight, but she was staring out of the window and didn't seem to notice me. Flynn and Leo were still sitting silently side by side. Flynn was drumming his fingers on the table. Leo shuffled uncomfortably in his chair.

I sat down. 'What happened, Flynn?' I asked. 'How was it?'

Flynn shrugged. He stared, pointedly, at Leo. It was obvious he didn't want to talk in front of him.

So much for hoping he would open up.

Leo cleared his throat and got up. 'I have to . . . do something in my room . . .' He left the kitchen.

'What's wrong?' I said.

Flynn still said nothing. I turned to Gemma. The kettle had boiled and she was pouring water into a row of mugs. 'Gemma, what's the matter with him?'

Gemma glanced over. 'Not sure, honey. Hey, Flynn, tell her what happens next month.'

Flynn sighed. He raised his eyes at last. 'In four weeks' time, we have to bring someone who's been affected by our "negative behaviour",' he said grumpily. 'Which should be a laugh.'

'What does that mean?' I said.

'It means you have the chance to go to group counselling with Flynn,' Gemma said.

I frowned. That sounded like a positive thing. Why was Flynn so annoyed? 'Don't you want me to come?' I asked.

Flynn shrugged again. 'I guess it's fine,' he said.

My head spun. I couldn't work out what the problem was. But before I could try and get Flynn to talk about it some more, he had got up and walked outside. Resisting the urge to follow him, knowing he was best left alone for a bit, I turned to Gemma.

'What's going on?' I asked.

Gemma ran her fingers through her long black hair. 'I think it's just a lot for Flynn to get his head around, that's all.'

She set a tray of mugs on the table, as Dad and Ros and Leo's dad all came into the room. Dad and Gemma started talking about their day and I wandered over to the open door. Flynn was already on his way back to the kitchen, his head bowed. As I stood outside waiting, he looked up and smiled. The act transformed his face – like the sun coming out after a storm. He walked over and pulled me into a silent hug.

'Sorry,' he whispered.

'It's okay but what's the matter?' I said, feeling more confused than ever.

Instead of answering, Flynn went inside where Dad and the others were sitting around the table. I followed him indoors, still feeling troubled.

'You want to be careful with all that negative gender stereotyping,' Ros was saying to Leo's dad. 'You'll give Leo a complex. I mean, you're his primary role model, God help him.'

'If *he's* Leo's primary role model I don't think God's help will be anything like enough,' Flynn said as he crossed the room to the sink.

Ros roared with laughter. Leo's dad managed a thin smile. He nudged Ros with his elbow. 'Stop it.'

She nudged him back. 'Stop it yourself.'

Jeez, they were behaving like a couple of little kids.

I caught Flynn's eye as he poured himself a glass of water. He shook his head.

'Hard work, isn't it?' Gemma said, wandering over with a cup of peppermint tea in her hand.

I wasn't sure whether she was referring to the group counselling Flynn had just come back from, or having to listen to Ros and Leo's dad.

Flynn shot a resigned smile at her.

'Have you been to your evening class?' Leo's dad said, also coming over. 'How was that, son?'

I froze. The smile slid off Flynn's face. I knew he hated being called 'son' almost as much as he hated being asked questions about his counselling sessions. The other residents all knew Flynn attended them but, so far, they'd been tactful enough not to pry.

Flynn cleared his throat. 'We were exploring issues of anger, identity and belonging,' he said in a high-pitched, slightly nasal, American accent.

Gemma stifled a giggle. I guessed Flynn had just done a good imitation of Sally, the woman who led his group counselling.

'Oh, aye,' Leo's dad said. 'And what's that about when it's at home?'

'Stuff about how important it is to have roots, to belong somewhere, to know where you come from.' Flynn sounded bored but I could feel his body tensing. He was hating being questioned. *Jeez*, suppose he started getting cross . . . lashing out?

'We have to go,' I said suddenly, taking Flynn's hand.

Ignoring the surprised look on Leo's dad's face, I led Flynn out of the room and up the stairs. He didn't protest and we didn't speak until we reached the corridor leading to Dad and Gemma's rooms.

I dropped Flynn's hand and leaned against the wall.

'Thanks for getting me out of there,' Flynn said. His eyes were soulful in the dim light that seeped out from under the closed doors down the corridor. 'I'm sorry I was so . . . so down before.'

'So . . . what do you think about all that stuff . . . about where you come from and where you belong?' I asked. I wasn't sure what I wanted to know, I was just hoping Flynn would tell me more about the counselling session . . . especially if I was going to be coming along in a few weeks' time.

Flynn pulled me closer towards him. 'I belong here.' He put his hand on my face. I closed my eyes as his fingers stroked my cheek. 'Nothing else matters,' he whispered, pulling me towards him. 'Okay?'

'Okay.' I hugged him back.

This was how I loved him best. When his black mood evaporated and his whole being was focused on me . . . loving me, needing me. In those moments I felt whole.

A creak on the stairs.

I opened my eyes to see a flash of blond hair disappearing around the corner.

'What was that?' Flynn asked.

I was certain it was Leo. Had he been watching us? I didn't want to spoil Flynn's loving mood so I just shrugged.

'No idea,' I said, then I led Flynn into our room.

11

Two days before sixth form college started I went back to Mum's for a visit. I'd been to see her every couple of weeks since I'd come to live at the commune, but I usually only stayed one night, and now Flynn and I were living together, I didn't even really want to do that. It was so clear Mum disapproved of Flynn and me being together that, even if she didn't say anything, the atmosphere in the house was always strained. Still, both Mum and Dad insisted I went.

It was weird the way Mum's house no longer felt like home. Mum had moved my remaining things into Stone's old room. She tried to make it look nice, hanging up a print I used to like and putting a pretty throw over the bed, but these things just made the room feel even less personal to me. I lay on the bed, gazing at the faded blue of the walls and the little dark stains where Stone's posters had been stuck on with Blu-tack, and found myself feeling homesick for the commune.

At least it was fun seeing Emmi and Grace that evening. Emmi had spent a fabulous month in France and had, naturally, acquired a fantastically good-looking French boyfriend. He certainly looked gorgeous in the many pictures Emmi had taken of him on her phone. For a couple of hours it was Jean-Luc this and Jean-Luc that, then he actually called and Emmi squealed and they had a long flirtatious conversation – in English – about when he was supposed to be arriving the following week.

'Of course we can,' Emmi said. She was standing out on the landing, her mobile clamped to her ear. 'And we have nice bread here in England as well, you know.'

Grace and I settled down on Emmi's bed. We were painting our toenails, waiting for Emmi to come back. I was enjoying being girly after a long week tending the commune's vegetable patch.

I raised my eyes. 'Sounds like Jean-Luc's as high maintenance as our Em.'

'So how's it going living with Flynn?' Grace asked. 'My parents would *never* let me have James come live with us.'

I shrugged. 'It's not like we're living in a family home, remember. We're part of the commune,' I explained, stroking nail varnish over my big toenail. 'But I love being there with Flynn.'

Grace and I chatted for a bit about what we'd been doing. Grace had gone to a festival with James since I'd last seen her. Flynn and I could have gone with them but Flynn hadn't had the money and I wasn't sure I really wanted to go anyway. It sounded like Grace and James had had a great time. Grace told me about some of the bands they'd seen, then she blushed.

'I know I said I wouldn't mention it again but did you ever tell Flynn about what happened with James? James asked me to ask you.'

I shook my head. 'No way,' I said. 'Flynn would never understand.'

'You mean he wouldn't believe you and James hadn't wanted to kiss each other?'

I shrugged. 'He'd just be mad at the idea of it.'

Grace screwed the top back on her nail varnish bottle. 'D'you think he might wonder if the pair of you secretly like each other?' Her fingers trembled as she set the bottle down.

'Oh, Grace . . .' Was that what *she* thought? 'You don't . . . James and me . . . *no* . . .' My stomach twisted into knots. I hadn't thought about James and me since the last time I'd seen Grace. Had she been worrying about it all this time?

'It's just been on my mind a bit.' Grace's voice dropped to a whisper though there was no chance of us being overheard; Emmi was still chatting away on the landing to Jean-Luc, her phone clamped to her ear. 'I realised I was grateful that you hadn't, you know, gone any further with him.'

What? My mouth dropped open. 'No. James didn't *want* me, Grace. It wasn't like that. And I didn't want him. Not that he isn't lovely but—'

'If you'd wanted to, I bet he'd have done it.' Grace's mouth trembled. 'I mean, the way you look, what guy wouldn't want you?'

'You're kidding.' I stared at her, genuinely amazed. 'James is totally in love with you. Anyway, you're ten times prettier than I am. Look at you. You're like a supermodel.'

Grace shook her head. 'I'm not like you and Emmi,' she said matter-of-factly. 'It's fine, Riv, but I've seen the way guys look at you. I know James loves me but it would still be tempting for him . . . that's all . . .' She tailed off, looking miserable.

I hugged her, feeling simultaneously confused and relieved and guilty. How could Grace think for a second that James would be interested in me, when he had her? Is that what Flynn would think, if he knew? That I was secretly all into James?

I drew back. 'I swear James has never done

anything to make me think he liked me like that,' I said. 'And you can tell him that I haven't said anything to Flynn.' I paused. 'And that I really don't want him to say anything either.'

'Sure,' Grace said. 'But maybe Flynn would be more understanding than you think?'

I shook my head. 'No way.' If sensible, sweet-natured Grace had got upset at the possibility of James and me fancying each other then what on earth would passionate, volatile Flynn make of it?

12

I went back to the commune the next morning. College was going to start the next day and Gemma took me into Norton to buy a jacket. The shops here weren't anywhere near as cool as London stores but it was fun hanging out with Gemma. The more time I spent with her and Dad, the more I appreciated how lovely she was, like a still pool of water, keeping calm in the face of all storms. I'd even plucked up courage to ask her about losing her baby earlier in the year. There were tears in both our eyes as Gemma confessed she had cried recently, thinking how the baby would have been due around now. She also admitted that she and Dad were hoping she would get pregnant again soon, though she was eager to reassure me that no new arrival would ever take precedence over me and Stone. I came home, back to the commune, really hoping, for the first time, that Gemma and

Dad would have a baby. A little brother or sister would be so cool.

The next morning, Flynn, Leo and I took the bus to the sixth form college for our first day. Before we left, Dad gave me a peck on the cheek then turned to Flynn. 'Look after her,' he said.

It was just a small thing but it was nice that he said it.

Flynn nodded. His expression didn't change but I could tell he was pleased too. He and Dad had really bonded over the summer. I'd seen them many times working silently and happily together on shared jobs like mending the fence in the south field or checking over the sheep.

Flynn took my hand as we got off the bus. Leo walked behind us as we strolled along the street and into Norton Napier College. The main building was square and modern with clean, concrete walls. I'd liked it as soon as I'd seen it for the first time earlier in the summer: all the rooms smelled of fresh paint and were laid out as a grid, with clear signposts everywhere.

Flynn, Leo and I found our way easily to the secretary's office, despite the corridors teeming with teenagers. I knew there were only 180 students or so in the whole school – ninety in each year – but it felt like all of them were swarming past us. I noticed most of the girls were taller than me – and almost all wearing jeans or sweatpants. I was glad I'd put my jeans on rather than a skirt, and that I was wearing a simple black jumper – nothing too showy or obvious. Flynn looked cross, which I knew meant he was feeling a bit awkward, but he was still chatting quite normally to me. Of the three of us, it was Leo who was having the worst time. I glanced at him as Flynn opened the secretary's office door. He was actually shaking.

'Hi,' Flynn drawled. 'They said we should come here.'

'I'm Mrs McCudden.' A short, plump woman with wispy grey hair and a harassed expression bustled over to meet us. She shook our hands, then asked for our names. She found me and Leo on the lower sixth list straight away. 'Yes, River Armstrong and Leo Maxwell. No need to be nervous.' This was directed at Leo, who had gone white as a sheet. She handed us each a form. 'Just an extra bit of paperwork, then down to the hall for your induction.'

Leo and I sat down on the sofa with our forms. They were straightforward questions asking about contact numbers and checking home addresses. Two girls and a boy on the sofa opposite were filling in forms too. One of the girls looked up and smiled at me.

Mrs McCudden turned to Flynn. 'And your name is . . . ?'

'Flynn,' he said.

'Ah . . .' Mrs McCudden reached for another list. 'Upper sixth . . . Patrick Flynn. Is that right?'

'Just Flynn.' Flynn glared at the unfortunate Mrs McCudden.

She blinked distractedly. 'Sorry?'

'Just Flynn,' he repeated slowly. 'My name. Flynn. I'm not writing Patrick on anything.'

'Whatever you like, dear.' Mrs McCudden handed him a form, then bustled back to her desk.

A minute later we were all done. Leo and I joined Flynn as he handed his form in.

'So the three of you live on a commune?' Mrs McCudden said brightly. 'That must be interesting?'

Flynn ignored her. Leo looked down at the form he'd been filling in as if he might be sick all over it.

'That's right.' I smiled. 'Just a couple of miles away. My dad's been there a while.' Mrs McCudden and I chatted for a few minutes about what living on the commune was like. Then the door swung open and a young Asian man with glasses and sleek black hair peered round.

'Patrick Flynn?' he said.

Mrs McCudden bustled out from behind her desk again. 'This is Mr Shukla,' she said to Flynn. 'Your tutor.'

Mr Shukla grinned and held out his hand to Flynn.

'Hi, Patrick.'

'Flynn,' said Flynn, crossing his arms and looking mutinous.

I held my breath. I had often wondered how Flynn had managed to get every person at his old school to call him by his last name. Now the answer was obvious. He simply intimidated them into it.

'O-kay, Flynn,' Mr Shukla said, still holding out his hand.

Flynn shook it very briefly, then picked up his bag and slung it over his shoulder. He glanced at me. 'See you later, yeah?'

I nodded. He disappeared out the door. A moment later Mrs McCudden directed me, Leo and the other lower sixth students present to the hall. The whole year was here. After a short talk from the head, we were divided into four tutor groups. I was very relieved that Leo and I were in the same one. I gave Leo – who still looked very nervous – a reassuring smile as our tutor intro-duced herself as Ms Ransome from New Zealand. She seemed really nice – young and friendly – and wore a tight angora jumper that I couldn't have imagined on any of my old teachers at Langton. I liked her immediately. Leo, I noticed, didn't appear able to meet her eyes.

After Ms Ransome had checked us all against a register, she led us down the corridor to our tutor room. Having a surname beginning with 'A' meant, as usual, I was at the head of the line.

'So you live on the commune?' Ms Ransome asked, as we walked along. 'I've heard about it but I've never met anyone who lived there before.'

I started in on a repeat of the conversation I'd had earlier with Mrs McCudden. As we went inside our tutor room, Leo caught up with me and whispered, 'D'you think anyone's going to talk to us about anything other than living on a commune?'

His face was even paler than usual, his eyes still sick with fear, but at least he was smiling.

I grinned back. 'It's not that bad,' I said. 'Don't sweat it, we've got each other, remember.'

Leo nodded gratefully, as Ms Ransome asked us to sit. The tutor room wasn't anything like the old-fashioned classrooms at Langton. A row of lockers stood along one wall, with shelves opposite and a horseshoe arrangement of tables and chairs in between. Leo and I sat together, as Ms Ransome explained that the college was closely linked to the local comprehensive, which meant all but a handful of lower sixth students had come from the same school. I gulped when I heard this. I'd kind of assumed that everyone in our year would be strangers but it was already obvious most of the other students knew each other well.

'You'll use this tutor room for general studies and free periods,' Ms Ransome went on. 'And now I'm going to ask everyone to introduce themselves. Just a name will do at this stage.'

I felt nervous but when it came to my turn to say my name no one looked at me oddly. In fact, as I gazed around the room, I felt more confident than I had all morning. The tutor group was about twenty strong, half-half boys and girls. The girls were watching me, mostly with open, fairly friendly expressions on their faces. This was encouraging and I forced my mouth into a hint of a smile. The boys seemed to be giving their attention equally to me and Ms Ransome's chest. All except Leo, who spent the entire session staring at his shoes.

Ms Ransome gave out maps and timetables, then we headed off for our first lessons and the rest of the morning passed in a blur. I went to meet Flynn in the cafeteria at lunchtime. The college let you come and go as you pleased outside lesson times but Dad had given us tokens to buy a meal from the canteen on our first day. For the future, Flynn and I planned to go out as much as possible and bring our own food to eat in the local park.

The cafeteria was heaving when Leo and I walked in. I looked around, trying to make Flynn out. And then he was there, beside me, pulling me into a kiss.

I pushed him away, blushing.

'Missed ya,' he grinned.

I rolled my eyes, then noticed a small cut on his lip that hadn't been there this morning. 'What happened?' I stared at him. Surely even Flynn couldn't have got into a fight in just one morning?

Flynn's grin deepened. 'Just a bit of pushing and shoving. There're a couple of jerks in my class who think somebody new starting is an opportunity for them to assert their inner idiot.' He glanced at Leo, acknowledging his presence for the first time. 'Same in every class I 'spect.' He turned back to me. 'Don't look like that, Riv, it wasn't anything.'

'But you're hurt,' I said, all my old anxieties rearing up. Had Flynn lost his temper?

'Nah, I'm fine.' Flynn touched the cut on his lip. 'It's just a scratch. Look. It's freakin' dog eat dog out there. Most of them have been at school together since they were eleven – and they've *all* been here the whole of last year. I'm the only new person in my upper sixth tutor group. You can't let them think you're afraid. Not for a second.'

He dragged me over towards a queue for sandwiches and started fishing in his pocket for the tokens Dad had given him. 'I'm starving.'

I looked at him, still feeling troubled. 'I thought the anger management classes were going to stop you doing things like this,' I said.

'Things like what?' Flynn laughed, picking up a ham and mustard sandwich. 'I told you. It was just a bit of pushing and shoving. Me making sure nobody's going to start having a go at me in the future.' He leaned down suddenly. I could feel his breath, hot and steady, as his lips brushed across my ear. 'It's a one-off, Riv,' he whispered. 'Seriously nothing to worry about.'

We ate our lunch on our own. Leo had vanished somewhere between us buying our sandwiches and finding somewhere to sit down. I saw a few guys give Flynn wary looks. I was sure a small group of girls on the other side of the room were talking about us too. They kept looking over, then giggling and whispering.

I swallowed uncomfortably. I'd been at the same school for years before coming here. But even if I had moved around every term I was pretty certain that I would never draw attention to myself in the way that Flynn always seemed to.

Sometimes – if I was really honest – I didn't understand him at all.

13

As the first week turned into the second, we gradually settled into life at Norton Napier. I really liked Ms Ransome, who was the English and Drama teacher as well as my tutor. Mr Shukla turned out to teach History. He was strict but fair. I thought his lessons were a bit boring, though Flynn seemed to enjoy them – and to get on with Mr Shukla himself. In fact, Flynn got on with all his teachers. As he'd promised, there had been no repeat of the 'pushing and shoving' from our first day. And, like me, Flynn enjoyed the way Norton Napier allowed its pupils far more independence than either of our previous schools had done.

The other students were mostly nice too. I made friends with one of the few girls who hadn't grown up in the area. Kirsty was small and red-haired and her family had just moved here from Scotland. We quickly got in with the main group of girls in the tutor group and spent quite a lot of time doing girly stuff like trying on each other's make-up in the bathrooms at break time.

I wished Leo could have made some friends. But his weirdness seemed to stand out even more at college than it did at the commune. To be honest, he and I didn't really spend much time together. We only took English classes at the same time. Our other subjects were different, and I spent most of my free time with either Flynn or the girls I'd made friends with.

Flynn didn't make any close friends, not that he seemed bothered. Instead he hung out with a largish group of boys from his class, spending most of his time when he wasn't working or with me playing football in the park close to the college.

Part of me missed my old school and Emmi and Grace, especially on my birthday, which took place halfway through our second week. At Langton all my friends would have remembered the date and made a fuss of me. Here, no one knew except Flynn and Leo and I insisted they promise not to tell anyone at college; it was just too early in the term for me to put myself forward like that.

It really didn't matter. We had a good time at the commune that evening. Mum and Stone came up for tea and Gemma baked a big chocolate cake. I got money for clothes from Mum and Dad, a book from Leo and a pretty pair of earrings from Flynn. Both Grace and Emmi called and texted too with promises of presents when we next met.

It felt a bit weird. Still, being here – at the commune and at the college – was what I had wanted. According to Emmi and Grace everything was different at Langton now anyway.

And, here, I had Flynn.

Before we knew it, the first four weeks had passed and it was time for me to attend Flynn's group counselling class with him. That evening we stayed late after college, then walked up the road to the Norton Therapy Centre. I was feeling really nervous at this opportunity to join in tonight. I'd asked both Gemma and Flynn what to expect but Gemma just said it would be better not to have preconceptions while Flynn wouldn't talk about it at all.

'I don't know, Riv,' he said. 'Sometimes it makes sense. Sometimes it's like we're all just talking about nothing.' He paused. 'Still, I'm sure it helps.'

The room the session was held in was like a big school hall, with a scuffed wooden floor and a bunch of plastic chairs arranged in a circle.

I sat down next to Flynn. He held my hand,

looking bored. My heart was thumping, I was so worried I was going to do or say the wrong thing. Most of the other people in the group were already there. They were all boys, Flynn had told me, between the ages of fourteen and eighteen. Most seemed to have come with their mothers, though a few were with their girlfriends and a couple with their dads. At least there was no one here from Norton Napier.

I shivered. Flynn squeezed my hand. 'Don't worry, Riv,' he said. 'There's nothing to be nervous about.'

A moment later the counsellor, Sally, turned up. She was about Mum's age, wearing jeans and a tunic top. She had short, spiky hair held off her face with a long purple scarf.

'Hi, everyone,' she drawled, in an American accent just like the one Flynn had imitated the other day. 'I'm real pleased to see you all. Tonight we're going to focus on the effects of anger on those around us and as part of the process I would like each of the guests here tonight to tell the person they came here with how their anger has impacted on their lives.'

I gulped. Was I going to have to speak in front of all these people? Flynn leaned over and whispered in my ear. 'You can say anything you like, Riv. I know what to do.'

I frowned, not sure what he meant.

But Sally was already asking the first person to speak.

It was one of the mums. Like most of the other parents in the room, she was drawn and tired-looking, with an anxious expression on her face. Her son, who looked about fourteen, sat beside her, slouched in his chair. He didn't look up as she spoke in a trembling voice, explaining how his temper had led to the break-up of her relationship with her boyfriend, and how she felt torn between loving her son and being scared of him.

After a little gentle probing from Sally, the woman admitted her son had hit her several times when she tried to stop him going out with mates she didn't approve of. Then Sally turned to the son, who'd sat sullen and silent the whole time. She asked him how hearing what his mum had to say had made him feel.

He grunted, 'Dunno.' Eventually Sally got him to admit he did feel bad after hitting his mum, though he kept saying he thought it was partly his mum's fault for winding him up. 'Because once I'm off on one, there's nothing that'll stop me. It's, like, not my fault. You can't control it.'

At this Sally smiled and started talking about responsibility. She explained how everyone had to own their anger. How if you blamed someone else for winding you up what you were really saying was that they were in control of you, instead of you being in control.

The boy nodded but I didn't get the impression he'd really understood what Sally was saying. She moved on to the next boy. He was older, more like Flynn's age, and one of the few here with his dad. But it was the same story. The boy lashing out and physically hurting his family for no really good reason that I could see. Despite being a few years older, he was just as tongue-tied as the first boy.

As Sally went round the room, I realised they were all the same. An uncomfortable pressure settled on my chest. Flynn didn't belong here. He had never once hit his family, well, apart from his dad, of course. Nor me. And he understood himself far better than these other guys. For the first time I questioned whether being here could really help him. Still, Flynn had said it did.

My heart pounded as it got closer and closer to my turn to speak. I hardly heard what the people sitting next to us said; all I could think about was what I was going to say. I glanced at Flynn. He was still holding my hand but he hadn't made eye contact while differ-ent people were telling their stories. Right now he was yawning, staring at the floor. I wondered what he was thinking. How he was feeling.

'River, is it?' Sally's voice brought me back to the room. I looked up, my face flushed. Everyone was gazing at me.

I nodded at Sally. She smiled. 'Flynn has mentioned you in our sessions before.'

I looked sideways at him. He raised his eyes and gave me this hard, sexy, ironic look. I gulped, wondering what he had said.

'So, River,' Sally went on. 'Perhaps you would like to share with the group a time or a feeling to do with Flynn's behaviour.'

'Right.' My mind was blank. I stared at my hand, still in Flynn's.

What on earth was I supposed to say?

14

'I realise this is a difficult situation for you, River,' Sally said encouragingly. 'But please know that you are in a safe environment. Nothing you say here will go outside the room.'

I stared down at the floor.

'I reckon she's scared of him.' This came from one of the few other girlfriends in the room. A fat, blonde girl in a ridiculously short skirt. She'd already talked about her boyfriend's jealousy and how he was always threatening guys if he thought they'd been trying it on with her.

Sally cleared her throat. 'Can you tell us how you are feeling, River?'

I wanted to crawl under my chair and curl up.

'*Are* you feeling scared?' Sally's voice grew softer, more sympathetic. 'Because you know this is a safe space and Flynn can't—'

'I'm not scared of him.' I looked round the room.

'*Really*,' I said. 'I'm not scared, it's just hard to remember something. Flynn's never hurt me. He's only ever hurt other people – and mostly only when they've provoked him.'

I could feel Flynn looking at me. I kept my eyes on Sally. She was frowning.

'You mean he's never hurt you physically?'

'That's right.'

Sally smiled. 'Okay, then how about you tell us about a situation you've been in where Flynn's response has . . .' she paused, '. . . made you feel *uncomfortable*.'

My chest tightened. 'Well . . . when he hit his dad that was horrible. But though his dad didn't really do much at the time, it was still provocation . . . because of what he'd done to Flynn before . . . so I understood.' I stopped, not wanting to go into the details of Flynn's relationship with his da. Sally nodded at me. I was sure she knew what I was referring to.

'What about another occasion when you were there and Flynn lost his temper?' Sally asked.

My mind flitted over the many times when I'd seen Flynn get angry. I took a deep breath.

'There was this one time when he found out about his sister's boyfriend.' I hesitated, embarrassed suddenly to share my feelings with this group of strangers. I looked at Sally, hoping she would interrupt and take over the conversation, but she didn't. Everyone waited for me to speak. Flynn squeezed my hand. I still hadn't looked at him.

'Well . . .' My voice was all shaky. 'What happened was that I found out Flynn's sister was with this guy, Gary, but she asked me not to tell anyone so I didn't. Then, one day, Flynn found out and he lost it and pushed Gary against the wall and threatened him.' I paused, remembering how terrified I'd felt at the time. 'I was really scared that Flynn would hit him and that there'd be a fight. There wasn't but when Flynn realised I already knew about Gary and Siobhan he got angry with me too. He shouted and said horrible things. Then he stormed out.'

'And how did that make you feel?' Sally asked.

I let out a long, slow breath. 'Scared, mostly. And upset. And guilty, because I thought maybe I should have told Flynn. But it would have been breaking a promise to Siobhan if I had, so . . .'

I looked down.

'How does it make you feel to hear all that, Flynn?' As Sally spoke, Flynn took his hand away from mine. Out of the corner of my eye I could see him sitting back and crossing his arms. 'It makes me feel bad that River was frightened,' he said. 'But I was

135

scared too that this guy I'd never met was going to hurt my sister.'

Sally nodded. 'Why would you assume he was going to hurt her?'

Flynn shrugged.

''S fair enough,' said one of the other boys. 'Guy's gonna do your sister, he's asking for a punch in the—'

'Thank you, Jason.' Sally sniffed. 'But I'd like Flynn to think about what I'm asking here.' She turned back to Flynn. 'Do you think your reaction was appropriate?'

I looked at Flynn for the first time. He was glaring at Sally, his arms still folded, his jaw clenched. When he spoke it was slowly and hesitantly, as if he was having to push every word out.

'I think I overreacted about Gary. I should have stopped and talked and found out about him first, though he was in my home and I wasn't expecting him and I don't think there's anything wrong with assuming someone's going to jump you if you don't know them. That's just how life is.'

There was a murmur of approval round the circle of boys. Sally's lips tightened slightly. 'And what about River?'

Flynn looked at me. He sighed. 'I still think I was right to be angry that River hadn't told me she knew about Siobhan and—'

'I promised Siobhan,' I blurted out, forgetting everyone else in the room. Flynn and I had never really talked about what had happened that day. We never really talked about anything like that. 'You couldn't expect me to break a promise.'

Flynn kept his eyes on mine. 'I didn't,' he said. 'I don't. I just think you shouldn't have made the promise in the first place.'

'But . . .'

'If I could come in here,' Sally said briskly. 'Rather than get bogged down in the ethics of the situation, let's focus on how else you could have handled it. Flynn, what else could you have said or done to express your anger that River had kept information from you?'

There was a short pause.

'I could have just told her I felt angry,' Flynn said. 'I could . . . I *should* . . . have said: "River, I understand that you made a promise to Siobhan but I'm your boyfriend and I don't want us to have secrets from each other." I wish I'd said that instead of shouting, because I hate River being upset and scared.'

Another pause. Flynn and I looked at each other. His eyes were bright and open, as vulnerable as I'd ever seen.

'And how would you feel if Flynn had said that, River?' Sally asked.

'Better,' I said, not taking my eyes off him. 'Yeah, I would have understood that.'

The rest of the session passed smoothly. I didn't say anything else. I'm not sure Flynn would have done either but Sally drew him into a couple of the discussions that took place later on. I wasn't really certain, but it seemed to me that she was trying to get Flynn to help the other boys understand what she was saying. As if they were more likely to listen to him or something. It was flattering, I guess, and Flynn certainly didn't seem to mind. In fact, I was amazed by how patient he was throughout the session. Most of the other boys got riled at some point or just ignored what was said to them. But once we'd had our turn, Flynn stopped looking bored and listened attentively. When he did speak what he said was so perceptive and reasonable that it took my breath away.

Gemma picked us up and we travelled home in silence. Neither of us wanted to talk about the session in front of her and, like Dad, Gemma was good at sensing that kind of stuff and not pushing it.

When we got back Leo was in the kitchen, bending over some homework. Flynn threw him an irritated look and said he was going for a walk. He'd started to do that quite a lot, after his counselling sessions. I'd rather he'd talk to me but I understood he needed a bit of time on his own. And he was never gone for long.

I sat down at the table with a cup of tea, and asked Leo what he was working on.

'Spanish.' Leo glanced up from his textbook. 'Did you know there's no direct translation for the word "embarrassed"? There's "verguenza" for "shame", or maybe "avergonzado" if you mean, more, "abashed", maybe. But nothing that properly means "embarrassed". D'you think that's because Spanish people don't feel embarrassed like we do?'

'Dunno . . . maybe. It's interesting.' I took a sip of tea, grinning to myself at Leo's earnestness. His blond hair was all ruffled and there was a gigantic ink smudge on his cheek. He looked like some absent-minded professor.

'This guy in my Spanish conversation class, today . . .' Leo went on. He had bent over his exercise book and was writing in tiny, careful lines. '. . . he was showing off in our "show and tell" session, talking about when he went to some big international football match, and he wanted to say he was embarrassed about England losing to some rubbish team but he didn't know the word, so he tried to blag it by making one up, which works sometimes with big words in Spanish 'cos they're often like the

139

English ones. So he said "estaba embarazada" which actually means "I was pregnant".' He chuckled.

I watched him write across the page. Normally I never noticed how Leo looked. But right now, sitting there all unself-conscious and caught up in his work, he looked, well . . . he looked cute. If only he didn't get so uptight about things, I was sure he'd find life so much easier. Maybe the first step was coming to terms with being gay . . .

'How are you?' I said softly. 'Have you talked to your dad?'

Leo stopped writing and looked up. His face reddened as he registered what I meant. 'No.' He seemed to shrink a little as if all the easy confidence he'd been infused with when I'd come into the room was seeping out of his body.

'I'm sorry. I just thought maybe it was hard for you at school and stuff.'

Leo shrugged. 'It's okay.' He looked away.

I started to get up from the table.

'I haven't told anyone else what I told you about me,' he said.

I sat back down, feeling uncomfortable. 'Oh,' I said. 'Right.'

Leo looked like he was struggling to say something else. He shook his head. I groaned inwardly. Why was it always this heavy with him? I fidgeted in my seat, wanting to get away, but worrying it might seem rude . . . that maybe he wanted a chance to say more about how he felt about being gay. Then Leo leaned forward, across the table.

'You've got something in your hair,' he said, reaching his hand out towards me.

The door from the garden opened. Leo snatched his hand back as Flynn stomped in. He stared at us sitting at the kitchen table. I looked back at him, my face flushing. Leo stared down at the table. The atmosphere in the room felt suddenly charged, like an electric current was surging through it.

'Hi,' Flynn said. There was a tightness in his voice.

I stood up, feeling guilty, though I hadn't done anything wrong.

'I'm going to have a bath,' I said. Without looking at either Flynn or Leo I left the kitchen and went up to our apartment. Neither Dad nor Gemma were there. I grabbed a towel and started running a bath.

As I came out into the living area, Flynn appeared in the doorway of the apartment, his fists clenched by his sides.

'I'm sorry about that stupid counselling session,' he said in a low, angry voice.

'It was fine,' I said. 'Honestly, it wasn't that big a deal.'

'Well, I *hated* it,' Flynn said. 'I can't bear everyone

hearing our stuff. I can't bear thinking how weak it makes me look.'

Weak? I shook my head. 'I don't think that.'

Flynn unclenched his fists. He walked over and took my hand in his. 'You would tell me if anyone . . . you know . . . if anyone ever tries to . . . with you. I mean, you wouldn't *not* tell me, just because you think I'd go after them, would you?'

I stared into his eyes. 'Is this about Leo, downstairs?'

A beat passed. Flynn nodded. 'Partly. I can see how he looks at you. He was doing something just now, wasn't he?'

I shook my head, wondering if I should break my promise to Leo and tell Flynn his fears were groundless, that Leo was more likely to fancy him than me. 'He was just getting something out of my hair.'

Flynn touched my hair himself, letting the strands run through his fingers. 'There's nothing *in* your hair, Riv. He was just trying to get closer to you.'

I pulled away from him, irritated. 'No, he wasn't.' Again, it was on the tip of my tongue to tell Flynn that Leo thought he was gay. Again, I held back. 'Leo didn't do anything. He's *never* done anything.' I walked away, across the room.

Flynn followed me. 'Okay, I'm sorry,' he said, reaching out for my shoulder. 'Forget Leo.'

I turned slowly round to face him.

'Forget Leo,' Flynn repeated, his eyes soft gold in the electric light, beseeching. 'Just promise that you'd tell me if *anyone* has ever come after you. Please?' He paused. 'Has anything ever happened that you *haven't* told me?'

I stood in front of him, feeling uncertain. Should I tell him about Slug Tongue and James? For a second I seriously considered it. But then, I thought, what was the point? It was all a long time ago now. Almost seven months. I took a deep breath.

'I'm not saying no one's ever tried to talk to me when you weren't there. But no one's ever gone any further. Because I don't want anyone else. And I've always made that clear. So guys have always backed off. Because I love you. Which I do even more after tonight.'

Flynn's eyes softened. He ran a finger down the inside of my bare arm. I shivered at his touch and pulled him close.

'I love you too, Riv,' he said.

We stood, looking into each other's eyes. I marvelled at the huge feelings that rose inside me when we were together. Not the old, out-of-balance emotions I used to have, back in the days before we lived together, when Flynn's temper was an issue and I wasn't sure how he really felt about me, but something much more pure and intense – and way more powerful.

How was it possible to feel this much for someone? It was like we were really one person.

For a second the thought made me feel terrified. Suppose Flynn took his love away?

'It's all about you,' Flynn whispered. 'Everything in my life. All about you.'

I smiled. I didn't need to be scared. Flynn felt just like I did.

I couldn't imagine anyone or anything ever breaking us up.

15

Another couple of weeks passed and Flynn and I settled into a comfortable routine. We were both busy and, what with our schoolwork and the chores at the commune, we had very little spare time. It was October now and the weather grew cooler as the days shortened. Flynn's eighteenth birthday took place in the middle of the month. Like me, he didn't want a big fuss made at college but Gemma and I baked him a cake which everyone shared after dinner. Flynn's mum sent him a parcel containing gifts from her and his sisters, and I gave him a practical present that I knew he really wanted – some new football boots.

After dinner, Flynn drew me to one side saying he had something to show me.

'What is it?' I asked as we went up to our room. 'Are you sure you liked the boots?' I'd been a bit anxious about them all week. They weren't the most romantic present.

'The boots are awesome, Riv,' Flynn reassured me. 'Come here.'

He led me over to the chest of drawers, opened the middle drawer where he kept his clothes and drew out a loop of thin leather cord. A tiny blue 'R' dangled from the end. It was the one from the broken chain, that Grace had given me years ago just after we started at Langton.

'I took it to be mended but it needed a whole new chain so I got this leather thong instead. It totally matches the "R", look.' Flynn held the necklace up so I could see the thread of blue that ran through the black leather. 'What do you think?'

I nodded. 'It's great but . . . but it's *your* birthday, you shouldn't be giving me presents.'

Flynn grinned. 'Who says?' He offered me the necklace. 'I think this leather looks awesome.'

I stared at him. 'Then you should wear it,' I said. I held up the bracelet he'd given me earlier in the year. 'You gave me this, I'm giving you that.'

'Really?' Flynn's eyes widened. 'Excellent.' He put the leather around his neck then tucked the 'R' down his shirt. 'Now you'll always be with me, see?' he said, making a silly face.

I grinned back. In the distance a firework exploded. There'd been quite a few going off recently late at night, people getting ready for Bonfire Night in a few weeks' time.

'Hey, let's have a party!' I said, suddenly consumed with excitement. 'For *both* our birthdays.'

Flynn frowned. 'What *here*? In the commune?'

'Yes.' I nodded eagerly. 'We can invite everyone from college and all our friends from our old schools.'

'I don't have any friends from St Cletus's,' Flynn said.

'What about James?' I said.

'Okay but . . .' Flynn looked out of the window as another distant firework exploded in the sky. 'Hey, d'you think your dad would let us build a bonfire?' He looked excited.

'For the party? I guess he might,' I said, confused by why Flynn seemed so thrilled. 'I was thinking we could have the party in the barn. Dad wants it cleared out anyway, and there's loads of room. Maybe we could borrow a sound system or—'

'That's a *brilliant* idea.' Flynn gave me a hug. 'Let's go and ask them now.'

We tore downstairs. Dad and Gemma were sipping cups of peppermint tea and chatting with Ros and John in the kitchen. It took a few minutes to persuade them that we should have the party. Flynn was great at batting away all the objections the adults raised: there wouldn't be any mess or any damage because we'd stay in the barn; we'd move the sheep to the top field and make sure no one went anywhere near them – or beyond, to the hens and the vegetable patch; and he'd set up a rota of people to guard the bonfire all evening.

'Please, Dad?' I asked, squeezing my hands together. 'I haven't had a party for years and Flynn's never had one and it's his eighteenth.'

Dad fetched the other residents: John's wife, Julia, the IT guy and Leo's dad. They had a small conference while Flynn and I waited anxiously outside. After about ten minutes, Dad emerged to say they'd all agreed, provided we agreed to their ground rules about drink and drugs and to oversee everything in a sensible and responsible way.

Flynn and I were ecstatic. We decided to hold the party at the end of the month, on the last Saturday of half-term. I pointed out to Flynn that this was also the date of our one-year anniversary. It seemed like a good omen and soon preparations were in full swing. I was in charge of invitations and soon had promises from almost everyone I asked at college and my old school that they were definitely going to be there. Gemma offered to cook a bit of vegetarian food, while Flynn talked to James about sourcing a sound system. Dad even said we could let our guests bring small amounts of cider. I grinned, wondering how he expected me to *stop* people bringing alcohol. It struck me that not having lived with me and Stone for so many years, Dad had missed out on a lot. Cider, indeed. I hoped the party could be outside as much as possible, where he'd be less likely to catch the inevitable flash of vodka bottles or smell the spliff.

Soon the only thing Flynn and I had left to do was clear out the barn. I was eager to get started but first I had to visit Mum. I caught the train to London straight after college ended for half-term, wishing I was still at the commune. I did want to see Mum, of course, but my head and my heart were in the place I'd left.

Mum picked me up from the station. She was cheerful and chatty as she drove me home. It was nice, actually, to sit in the kitchen and talk to her while she cooked tea and we waited for Stone to get back from football practice. When Mum told me he'd got a girlfriend I nearly fainted. How the hell had grumpy, smelly Stone managed to convince anyone to go out with him?

'Is she blind?' I asked.

'No.' Mum pursed her lips. 'Her name's Anna, and she's actually rather pretty. And *very* polite.'

I knew this was a dig at Flynn and my heart sank. Why did Mum have to make snide remarks when we were having such a nice time? I flushed, feeling annoyed, but before I could say anything, Stone himself walked in.

My mouth fell open. He'd been coming to the commune less and less over the summer and I'd hardly seen him at all since term started but I still wasn't prepared for the transformation before me. Gone was my slouchy, spotty little brother. In his place was a tall, clear-skinned boy with freshly washed hair that had been carefully gelled back off his scrubbed clean face.

'Hi,' he said.

'Hi.' I was so shocked that I ended up inviting him to the party next week. 'And you can bring your girlfriend,' I said, 'if she hasn't dumped you by then.'

Anna turned up about half an hour later. Mum insisted she came into the kitchen to meet me. Again, I was surprised. I'd kind of expected an ordinary-looking girl, probably fairly immature. But Anna was, like Mum had said, rather pretty, with straw-berry-blonde hair, a soft, round face and sparkling brown eyes. She sat and chatted with me and Mum for about ten minutes until Stone loped in. Then she blushed as he came over and put his arm round her.

'Let's go,' he said.

Anna looked up at him shyly. *Oh my goodness.* She was totally into him.

My mouth fell open as Anna got up from the table and said, ultra-politely, how nice it had been to meet me.

'How old is she?' I said, as soon as they'd left the room.

'Almost fifteen, like him,' Mum smiled. 'Nice, isn't she? Straightforward.'

This was a dig at Flynn *and* me. But this time I didn't feel like flying off the handle. Who cared what Mum thought? I had Dad and my friends. And Flynn.

I went around to Emmi's later. We sat in her bedroom with Grace, eating biscuits. Emmi was intrigued to hear about Stone's transformation.

'So would you say he was cute now, Riv?'

I screwed up my face. 'Ew, Emmi, I don't know. He's my brother.'

Emmi laughed, then told me she'd dumped Jean-Luc. 'He was so full of himself,' she explained. 'So demanding.'

'Sounds like you were made for each other,' I said with a grin.

Emmi rolled her eyes and threw a biscuit at me. 'Well, you can talk,' she smirked. 'Look at you and Flynn.'

I laughed and we chatted on. Emmi and Grace were full of tales about the boys they'd met recently: new friends of James and others. It all seemed a bit over the top to me but then they still went to a girls' school while I'd just spent nearly two months in a sixth form college where boys were an everyday fact of life.

Emmi and Grace went on for ages about people I didn't know and I started to feel a bit left out. I guess it showed in my face because, after a while, Grace squeezed my arm and said: 'It's not the same as being with you, though.'

'Yeah, girl. We miss you.' Emmi grinned. 'And there's a new guy we've met who'd be perfect for you.'

I stared at her. 'I already have a boyfriend, remember?'

Emmi shrugged and got up to go to the bathroom.

I watched her sashay out of the room, feeling mildly irritated.

'Why does she wind me up like that?' I said, chomping into a biscuit.

Grace shook her head. 'Cos she can?' she said. 'You wind her up just as much.'

That was true. I sighed, telling myself I shouldn't rise to Emmi's bait. She and I had always bantered with each other and she never meant any harm by it. Emmi just enjoyed saying things for effect.

'How's James?' I asked.

Grace's face lit up. 'He's good. We got together a year ago last week, you know.'

I nodded, remembering the party where that had happened, just a short while before Flynn and I started going out. I had thought Flynn didn't like me and drank so much I was sick. I could remember as clearly as if it had happened yesterday how Flynn had looked after me. How we'd stood outside and he'd rubbed my arms to keep them warm, then slid his fingers down my cheek and . . .

'River?' Grace grinned. 'I said, how's Flynn?'

'Okay. Better than.' I paused. 'I'm glad he and James still see each other.'

We talked for a while about the party. Grace and Emmi said they were sure loads of my old friends from Langton would be there. James, who had just had his own eighteenth birthday, had been given a car and was planning to drive Grace and Emmi to the commune. Emmi thought this was very cool, of course, but I could tell Grace was a bit nervous. She told us that James was under strict instructions from his parents not to drink at the party. Emmi rolled her eyes at that but Grace thought it was a good idea and was planning to limit her own intake to support him.

We chatted on; it was a laugh and I was in a good mood at the end of the evening when I went back to Mum's. She and I hung out together most of the following day. She took me shopping and we bought some new clothes – a couple of casual things for college and a new dress I was planning to wear to the party.

I headed home on Sunday morning, eager to see Flynn. I knew – from the commune rota – that he was due to work in the orchard that day. Dad and Gemma were out, so I caught the bus from the station. As soon as I arrived at the commune, I raced down to the orchard. It was chilly, just starting to rain. There was no sign of Flynn though his work, which involved raking the leaves in the orchard into huge, netted piles, had clearly been done.

I rushed inside and tore up to our flat. Flynn wasn't there. I wandered back downstairs. I'd seen Ros and Leo out by the hens. I'd go and ask them if they knew where he was. As I passed the living room, I heard the dull thud of a bass beat, the sound you get through headphones. I peered around the door.

Flynn was sitting at the table in the corner, papers spread out on the desk in front of him, his earphones clamped to his head. I crept up behind him, intending to surprise him with a kiss.

I peered over his shoulder to see what he was doing.

I froze.

University entrance papers.

We hadn't talked about where Flynn might go to uni since the summer holidays. I knew James was planning on staying in London to be near Grace. Please let Flynn want to do the same thing.

Flynn must have sensed me standing there, because he turned round. He tugged the earphones off his head and grinned. 'Hey, Riv.'

I was still staring at the forms on the table. 'What are you doing?' I said.

Flynn frowned. 'Just getting started on these,' he said. 'I have to apply soon. Mr Shukla made me do the Oxford one at school already.'

'Oxford?' My mouth felt dry. 'Where else are you applying?'

Flynn ran his hand through his hair. 'Dunno yet,' he said. 'I've got to check out the other courses but Oxford would be best. Or Cambridge but you can't apply to both at once, so . . .'

My eyes widened. I looked up at Flynn, an icy chill settling on my heart. 'Oxford?' I whispered. 'Cambridge?'

Flynn shrugged, misunderstanding me. 'I know it sounds mad but Mr Shukla thinks I could get in.'

I struggled with the feelings battling inside me. On the one hand, it was fantastic that Flynn was thinking about uni – and I was as sure as Mr Shukla that if he wanted to go to Oxford or Cambridge then he would certainly be offered a place. On the other . . .

'Oxford and Cambridge are so far away.' The words slipped out of me before I could stop them.

'Not really.' Flynn slid his arm around my waist. 'You could still visit. I could still come back and be with you.'

I nodded. 'Or you could study in London. There are loads of places to do law there and it would be much easier for us to see each other.'

'That's true,' Flynn acknowledged. 'But I want to go to the best place there is. Get the best degree I can. Everyone I've talked to says that the fastest way to earn loads of money in law is to get a degree from Oxford or Cambridge and then—'

'Money?' My eyes welled with tears. I'd heard his reasons for wanting to be a lawyer before. 'Is that all that matters to you?'

'No.' Flynn frowned at me. 'Don't get upset, Riv. Please. This is about respect and doing the best I can for myself. For my mum.' He squeezed my waist. 'For you.'

'Sure.' I knew I was being selfish but I couldn't help it. 'I'll see you later,' I said and left the room, tears blurring my vision.

16

I headed for the stairs, intending to rush up to the privacy of my bedroom. Then I remembered it was Flynn's room too. He could follow me up there at any point and, right now, I wanted to be alone, to sort through how I felt.

It suddenly struck me that, for the first time in my life, I had no room of my own. No place where I could be completely private. I veered away from the stairs and raced out the back door. I ran across the field, past the sheep towards the barn which Flynn and I were due to spend the next couple of days clearing out. Tears streamed down my face. I didn't really understand why I was so upset – after all, nothing bad had actually happened.

At last I reached the barn. It was an old building with a high ceiling and a loft that jutted out over the floor. Once, Dad had told me, it had been a hay barn but for the past ten years the residents of the commune had used it as a general dumping ground. The most accessible areas of the ground floor were still used to store farm equipment and tinned food but most of the rest of the dusty floor was covered with junk. I raced past the old paint tins, rusting hoes and scraps of wire netting and hauled myself up the ladder and onto the loft platform. I curled up beside a pile of broken chairs. It was still light outside but my corner was dark and draughty. I buried my head in my arms and wailed.

In my heart I knew it wouldn't be the end of the world if Flynn went away to uni next year but it felt like we'd only just settled into life on the commune – and I couldn't bear the thought of it being disrupted again. I cried for a few more minutes, then lay, sniffing, my arms wrapped around my chest.

After about half an hour, I was stiff and cold. I sat up, wiping my eyes and thinking about going back inside.

'River?' Gemma's voice echoed around the barn. Footsteps sounded below me.

'River, are you in here?' That was Ros.

I crawled out from behind the broken chairs and peered down. Ros saw me immediately. 'Hey.' She smiled. 'No guy's worth this many tears.'

'Sweetheart.' The sound of Gemma's gentle

concern brought more tears to my eyes. I somehow made my way down the steps and stumbled into her arms.

She held me, stroking my hair. 'Sssh, now,' she whispered. 'Sssh.'

She led me over to a battered old shelving unit covered with ancient gardening tools. An old sofa with the stuffing leaking out of stained cushions rested against the wall. Gemma sat me down and took the seat beside me while Ros perched on the arm.

'This is filthy,' Ros said with a grimace. 'Definitely one for your bonfire.'

Gemma squeezed my arm. 'Flynn was looking for you, River. He couldn't find you in the house. Thought you might be out here. We said we'd come and see.'

I nodded and Gemma put her arm round me. 'He told us why you're upset.'

I rested my head against her. 'He did?'

She nodded. 'Yup. You don't want him to leave London to do his law degree next year. Is that right?'

'Well . . .' Hearing Gemma say it out loud like that, it sounded really mean and childish. I swallowed. 'It's not so much that I mind him leaving, as that I'll miss him. I mean, maybe he isn't as into me as . . . as he makes out.'

Ros snorted. 'I'd like to see how he behaves when he *is* into someone then. He never takes his eyes off you.' She paused, grinning. 'Or his hands.'

Gemma squeezed my arm again. 'It's true, you know, River. I think he really does care about you. He was ever so upset when we found him looking for you. He was even saying he would stay in London.'

I sat up. 'Really?'

I looked from Gemma to Ros.

Ros frowned. 'But we told him not to.'

'What?'

'That's right, River.' Gemma cleared her throat. 'It's not right for you to stop Flynn studying where and how he wants to.'

'I know.' I looked away.

'Listen, River.' Ros turned my face towards her. 'It's a miracle Flynn's still going to school, given his background. The fact that he's bright enough and working hard enough to possibly get on the best courses in the country – that's something you should support him doing.'

'I do,' I insisted. 'It's just hard to think of him being so far away. Anyway, he only wants to be a lawyer to get rich and have people respect him.'

Ros sighed. 'Look, Flynn's got a lot of growing up to do,' she said. 'He may change how he thinks. And he won't be in a position to get a job like that for years. And anyway, even if he does get some hotshot corporate position, I think I'd rather have somebody like him, who understands how tough life can be, than some stupid rich kid who's only where he is because Mummy and Daddy pulled some strings.'

'Don't make this about you, River,' Gemma said. 'If you really love Flynn then you'll let him make his own decisions. It doesn't mean you have to stop seeing each other. I mean, if you and him are meant to last then you'll find a way through.'

I knew she was right. I didn't say anything as we tramped through the chilly air back up to the house. Once inside, I went up to our room. Flynn was lying on the mattress, reading a book. He sat up when he saw me.

'Riv?'

There was such love and tenderness and concern in his eyes that my own filled with tears again. I walked over to him and lay down. We held each other for a minute. I laid my head on his chest and let myself sink against him. His leather cord – and the tiny 'R' on the end of it – dug into my cheek.

'I came to look for you but they told me to leave you alone for a bit. That you needed some time. So I waited here.' Flynn stroked my hair. 'Is everything okay?'

I closed my eyes. 'Everything's fine,' I said.

'I don't have to apply to Oxford or Cambridge,' he said. 'I bet they're full of idiots anyway.'

'No.' I looked up at him. 'You should go for the courses you want,' I said. 'We'll work it all out when we have to.'

Flynn gazed at me for a long time. Then he kissed my mouth. 'You look so beautiful.'

I smiled. 'So I guess when you go away to uni you'll stop having counselling sessions.'

'Man, I hope I can stop before then.' Flynn made a face. 'Your dad made me promise to go for a year which is up in March, if you include the one-to-one sessions I was doing before we moved here. I know I have to do the therapy thing until then or he'll kick me out of the commune but after that . . .'

I frowned, suddenly realising how weird it was that Flynn felt his home was conditional on attending weekly counselling. 'I don't think my dad would kick you out just for that,' I said. 'I mean, where would you go?'

Flynn shrugged. 'I guess I'd have to get a job and a flat like I'd planned before we came here.'

I lay still, thinking what that would be like. 'Is it scary?' I asked. 'You know, worrying that if you do something wrong you'll lose your home?'

'Not really. It's like . . . the commune isn't my

home. It's just a building where I hang. And Mum's house isn't my home either, now.'

'Isn't it?'

'Nah.'

'So . . . so don't you feel you have a home then?'

'Course I do.' Flynn leaned over me, sliding his fingers over my face, lowering his lips to my neck. 'What d'you think you are?'

'It's still got a beautiful frame,' I said, holding up a small, gilt-edged mirror.

'But the glass is cracked,' Flynn said.

Dad nodded. 'He's right. It's trash, sweetheart. Pretty once. But useless now.'

I sighed and chucked the frame on top of the rubbish pile in the corner of the barn. It was the Wednesday afternoon before the party and Flynn and I had been clearing out the building since Monday morning. The job was far bigger than anyone had reckoned and it was looking increasingly unlikely that we'd finish without additional help so Dad and Leo had volunteered to pitch in along with Stone, who was visiting for a couple of days.

This was kind of Dad and Leo particularly, as they had already spent the entire morning creating a bin for leaf mould – the organic fertiliser that was formed from fallen leaves – out of tree stakes and chicken netting.

'Where on earth did all this stuff come from?' Dad muttered for the hundredth time.

It was amazing the amount of stuff various members of the commune had left in here over the years. In addition to the broken chairs I had curled up behind the other day, we'd found a set of warped tennis rackets, various board games half eaten by mice, several camping tables with the legs broken off, bits and pieces of furniture, clothes and baby toys, plus some old cans of paint.

One of the reasons the clear-out was taking so long was that Flynn and I often disagreed about whether a particular item was still useful or not. If it was it went into a separate pile and had to be stored away somewhere at the end of the day. Dad was partly here as arbiter between us and, so far, he'd taken Flynn's side on virtually everything.

It was hard going. I pushed my hair out of my eyes and delved into the next cardboard box. It was full of mismatched screws and nails.

'Rubbish,' I announced, dragging the box across the floor.

Flynn took a peek inside. 'No way, there's some usable stuff in here.'

Dad strode over and cast his eye. 'Yup. Plenty of

life in these. Leo can take them up to the house. I'll sort them out later.'

I rolled my eyes, stretching out the kinks in my back from all the bending over I'd been doing. As Leo left with the box, I looked around the barn. Dad, Stone and Flynn were now dragging a grubby single mattress out from behind a pile of old curtains. There was still an entire wall to be cleared but – once we'd got rid of the rubbish pile – there'd be miles more space in here than before.

We'd discovered a little alcove just to the right of the loft ladder which would be a perfect place to put the sound system. James had got some DJ friend of his brother to lend us his equipment and was planning to bring it over on Saturday afternoon. Grace and Emmi were going to come with him so the three of us could get ready for the party together. It was going to be just like old times. I couldn't wait.

'River?' Flynn emerged from behind the grubby mattress, beaming from ear to ear. 'There's a massive pile of wooden furniture back here. It's all broken and useless but it'll be perfect for the bonfire.'

'Great,' I said. I still wasn't sure quite why Flynn was so excited about the bonfire. James and Stone had been too, so maybe it was a boy thing. I mean, I thought the bonfire would be cool. But not *that* cool.

'Well, you can't burn this,' Dad said, dragging the

mattress towards the barn door. 'I'm going to take it up to the bins. We'll get the council to collect it later.'

As he left the barn, the mattress trailing behind him, Leo walked back in. He looked tired, not even glancing in our direction as he went over to the shelf he was clearing. Flynn picked up a pile of old curtain fabric. Dust swirled around him as he dumped the lot on the rubbish tip.

Stone, standing nearby, coughed, then drank some water from the bottle on the floor.

'So you seeing your girl when you get back home?' Flynn asked him.

I watched, amused, as Stone nodded and blushed. Even though he hadn't visited the commune all that much over the past few months, he'd still spent quite a lot of time around Flynn. It was obvious Stone had been a little intimidated at first but Flynn had made an effort to be friendly and the pair of them got on well now.

'What's she like, mate?' Flynn went on.

'Okay,' Stone mumbled. He was trying to sound cool, to impress Flynn, I realised.

'Only okay?' Flynn laughed. 'You can do better than okay, can't you?'

'I thought she was lovely,' I said, coming to Stone's rescue.

'Lovely *and* okay.' Flynn picked up the water

bottle and took a large gulp. 'Sounds a bit contradictory.'

'I expect she's beautiful,' Leo interrupted from across the barn.

We all turned to look at him.

'How would *you* know?' An edge crept into Flynn's voice.

Leo shrugged.

Ignoring them, I smiled at Stone. 'So are you going to bring Anna to the party?'

'I guess,' Stone said, his cheeks now purple.

'Course he is.' Flynn chuckled. 'Sorry, mate, I'm only teasing.'

Stone looked away but he was smiling and I sensed, as usual, that he didn't really mind Flynn's banter – that in fact he was flattered that Flynn had mentioned him having a girlfriend.

Leo, on the other hand, was gazing at Flynn with hatred. He sensed me staring and caught my eye.

'What is it?' I said, genuinely bewildered. Flynn hadn't said anything that harsh.

'Nothing.' Leo walked out of the barn.

'What's the matter with him?' Flynn asked.

I shook my head, feeling troubled. 'I don't know.'

17

The rest of the week passed in a rush. We worked late into the night on Friday, finishing our clear-out of the barn. While Flynn, Ros, Dad and Leo moved everything we were allowed to burn from the rubbish heap to the spot designated for the bonfire, Gemma helped me string fairy lights around the barn walls. We covered everything that was staying inside with tarpaulins and stood a couple of paraffin lamps on either side of the entrance. They cast a ghostly glow over the bare floors and walls.

The next day, Flynn and I slept late. We'd been let off chores for the day and, as soon as we woke up, Flynn darted outside to check on the bonfire pile. My phone was already full of texts and messages, mostly from my old mates at Langton, but also from newer friends at the sixth form college. For the first time I wondered how well everyone was going to mix.

I wandered downstairs and spent the next few hours helping Gemma put crisps into bowls and cook the veggie pizza squares she had made the day before.

I was in a state of high nervous excitement by three thirty, when James, Emmi and Grace arrived. James was driving his new car – a second-hand Honda. It wasn't a flashy motor by any means but it still seemed an amazing present. I couldn't imagine Mum and Dad ever being able to afford something like that for me. I watched Flynn let James have his moment showing the car off to us. At least my dad had always been there for me, unlike Flynn's da, who had done nothing but let him down. I don't think such thoughts occurred to Flynn himself. He was happy for James – and eager to try out the Honda. James took him for a quick drive while Emmi and Grace and I holed ourselves up in my bedroom to get ready for the party.

It was fun, just like I'd imagined. Emmi did Grace's hair, while Grace did my fingernails. Then Emmi started trying on her various outfits. This was always part of our routine – watching Emmi work her way through more and more outrageous clothes, while Grace squeaked with shock and I made cutting remarks about how Emmi's only aim in life was to attract boys, which made both the others laugh.

Tonight she looked stunning, even for Emmi. She was wearing staggeringly high-heeled boots and the tiniest shorts I'd ever seen. My stomach twisted as I looked at her. I'd always envied Emmi's legs and tonight they looked like they were going all the way to her armpits.

I stared down at my own outfit: a pale blue dress with a lacy pattern down the arms and across the middle. The dress was short – though longer than Emmi's shorts – and stylish but I still felt fat and frumpy beside her.

'That looks in*cred*ible, Em,' Grace squealed.

'Yeah, you'll have guys crawling all over you,' I said, trying to hide the jealousy in my voice.

'That's the idea,' she grinned.

A knock on the door. 'Can we come in?' It was Flynn.

I glanced at Emmi again. 'Sure.'

The door opened. Flynn and James walked in. They both looked great. Slicked-back hair, jeans and cool T-shirts. One stride into the room and they caught sight of Emmi. As if it was choreographed, they stopped together and stared.

Grace giggled. How could she be so relaxed about her boyfriend looking at someone else like that?

A sexy smile curved its way round Emmi's mouth.

'Hi, James,' she breathed. She looked at Flynn. 'Hi, Romeo.'

The knot in my stomach clenched tighter. I knew Emmi didn't really fancy Flynn. She didn't even really like him all that much. And she wasn't trying to upset me. She was just flirting because that was what she did.

James went bright red. Flynn just looked Emmi up and down. It was impossible to tell what he was thinking from the expression on his face. All my jealous feelings from a year ago flooded back. There they were: Flynn and Emmi, gorgeous and confident and . . .

'Looking good, Emmi,' Flynn said curtly. He turned to me. 'Can I have a word with you in private?'

I nodded, miserably.

'Fine.' Emmi sniffed. 'We know when we're not wanted.' She stalked out of the room, Grace and James right behind.

Flynn walked over. 'You okay, Riv?' He frowned.

For the first time I noticed that his hands were behind his back.

'I'm fine,' I said, trying to ignore the ugly, miserable feelings that twisted inside me. I pointed behind him. 'What have you got there?'

He grinned. 'Anniversary present.'

172

I stared at him. After initially acknowledging that the party would take place on our one-year anniversary, Flynn hadn't said anything further. I'd kind of resigned myself to the fact that he had either forgotten, or else thought it was too mushy and girly to make a fuss of. Either way, I knew Flynn had absolutely no spare money so . . .

'Don't you want to see what it is?'

I nodded, unable to speak. I couldn't believe Flynn was taking me by surprise like this.

Flynn brought his hands round from behind his back. Smiling, he pushed a small package into my hands. It was wrapped in blue tissue paper with loads and loads of different-coloured ribbons wound around the blue and spiralling off into curls.

'It's so pretty,' I gasped.

Flynn grinned. 'Gemma helped me with the ribbons. She showed me how to make them curl with a pair of scissors.'

I looked at him, tears in my eyes. 'Oh, Flynn.'

'You are such a nut job, Riv!' Flynn's grin deepened. 'You haven't even opened it yet.'

'I know.' I sniffed back the sob that was blocking my throat. 'It's just I saw you look at Emmi just now and she looks so fantastic and . . .'

Flynn rolled his eyes. 'Not this again. Look, Emmi

might have a great body but she's not so great on the inside. I mean, sorry, I know she's your friend but compared to you she's . . . she's . . .' He tailed off. 'She's not you, Riv. Nobody's you.' He put his hands on my waist. 'Now open my present.'

I fumbled with the ribbons. My hands were shaking slightly as I tore the last one off and ripped open the paper.

'Oh.' I sucked in my breath. In my hands was the old gilt-edged mirror Dad and Flynn had wanted to throw out with the rubbish from the barn. Somehow, Flynn had removed all the cracked glass from the mirror without damaging the pretty frame. And he'd replaced it with a picture of the two of us, then covered the photo with glass. I glanced at the back. A piece of wire had been threaded through the two metal loops so that it could be hung on a wall.

I turned the frame back over and stared down at our smiling faces. We were both wearing white shirts, sitting on the sofa at James's house, our arms wound round each other. I looked almost pretty, my eyes shining as I looked at Flynn. And he looked gorgeous. Handsome and loving and perfect.

'It's from one of those evenings we spent at James's. D'you remember? He and Grace kept taking pictures all night.'

I did remember. I remembered how happy I'd been that evening.

'I asked James to show me what he'd saved and he and Grace helped to pick out the best one . . .' Flynn bent down, trying to see my face. 'Do you like it?'

I looked up at him, my heart so full I could barely speak.

'It's the best present I've ever had since this.' I held up the silver heart bracelet on my wrist. 'I have a present for you too,' I said. I thought of the book of poems I'd bought him, which I'd wrapped and hidden in the barn earlier today. 'It's not as good as this but . . . I'll go and fetch it.'

But just then the doorbell rang and James shouted up to us to come down.

'Oh . . .' I said, disappointed.

'No worries, you can give it to me later,' Flynn said with a smile.

'Okay.' I propped the framed photo up on our chest of drawers and we went downstairs to find the others. James, Emmi and Grace were with Stone – who had clearly just arrived – in the kitchen. I looked around – there was no sign of Anna.

'Where's your girlfriend, Stone?' I asked.

He shrugged, looking uncomfortable. 'Er, that's over.'

'Are you okay?' I asked, feeling concerned.

'Yes,' Stone said, in a voice that made it clear he didn't want to talk.

'He's fine,' James said with a wink at me.

What did that mean? Had Stone *dumped* Anna? There was no time to find out because, right at that moment, the doorbell rang again. It kept ringing for about an hour, by which time most of our friends had arrived and I had got totally swept up in the bustle of taking everyone out to the barn, making sure the music was playing and sorting out the drinks.

I hardly saw Flynn for ages. All the adults, apart from Dad and Gemma, had left the commune for the evening and I spent a considerable amount of time showing my new friends from college around the house.

To my relief they were mostly impressed, saying how cool they thought it was. They liked the barn most of all. It did look pretty. We'd put up rows of party streamers alongside the fairy lights and they added soft pinks and oranges to the gentle glow.

By midnight the party was at its peak. The music was pounding out. The bonfire was raging. Some of the girls had complained that the fire was taking too many of the boys away from the dancing but apart from that everyone was having a brilliant time.

Dad and Gemma had gone upstairs half an hour

ago, after we'd let off the fireworks, with final, gentle warnings about not letting the fire or the music get out of control – so I no longer had to try and keep all the evidence of alcohol away from them. I'd only had a couple of drinks myself, though I could see loads of people were already fairly off their heads.

I chatted to James and Grace for a bit, telling them how much I liked the photo they'd helped Flynn choose for me. Emmi staggered over, clearly drunk. She was draped round one of Flynn's football mates from college who was grinning from ear to ear, his hand firmly clamped on her bum. As they started kissing, I wandered off, intending to find Flynn. I headed for the bonfire. It was still giving off fierce, hot flames that licked up into the sky.

Before I got halfway across the field, I heard someone cry out from the apple orchard. A male voice. '*No.*'

I looked around, but no one else was near me.

I turned and ran towards the trees. As I got nearer, I heard more voices. At least two others. And the same frantic voice I'd heard before.

'No, *please!*' It was Leo.

18

As I sped up, it occurred to me I hadn't seen Leo since Emmi, Grace and James had arrived. I felt a stab of guilt. Had Leo been hiding away from everyone all this time? I should have sought him out. I should have introduced him to some of my old friends.

'No!' Leo shrieked again.

And now what had happened? I darted through the trees, peering into the shadows. It was dark this far away from the house, the moon providing most of the light. And it was cold. I shivered in my dress.

I saw movement behind a tree and stopped, my heart thudding.

'*Please don't.*' Was Leo crying?

'You pathetic little freak.'

'Gay boy.'

I crashed through the leaves, past the tree. There in a clearing, half hidden down a slope, were two guys from Flynn's year. They were towering over a kneeling, shaking Leo.

All three of them turned and stared at me.

One of the guys from Flynn's class swore.

'Get lost, you stupid cow.'

I stopped running, shocked by the look of hatred on his face. I glanced at Leo. He was crying, his whole body trembling. At least he didn't look as if he'd been hurt. Yet.

The guy who'd spoken before took a step towards me. He raised his fist. 'I thought I told you to get lost.'

'Wait.' The other guy caught his arm. He leaned over. I could hear him whispering. A loud, drunken whisper.

'That's Flynn's girlfriend.'

The first guy looked startled. He dropped his fist and stumbled sideways. 'Right. Didn't mean nothing.'

'Come on, man.'

Together they raced off through the trees.

I stared after them, elated. I'd got rid of them. Well, the idea of Flynn had got rid of them. I didn't stop to think why it was that they should be so scared of Flynn. Or how they knew about Leo being gay.

I just raced over to Leo, who was still kneeling on the ground, clearly trying hard to stop crying.

'Hey.' I rubbed his back. 'Are you all right? Come on, let's go and get a drink.'

Leo staggered to his feet. 'Get off me,' he snarled.

I stood back, shocked. 'Leo?'

He tore past me and disappeared through the trees.

I wandered after him, slowly, out to the field. The bonfire flickered and glowed in the distance. Why was Leo so angry with me? I frowned, trying to puzzle it out. I'd risked my own neck to try and stop those guys attacking him, and he'd turned on me. It didn't make sense.

Unless.

The thought hit me with the force of a brick. Leo must have thought I'd told people he was gay. How else would those guys have known he suspected that he was? Leo had said he'd only spoken to me about it. Panic twisted in my chest. I had to find Leo and explain that I hadn't said anything. But there was no sign of him anywhere.

As I passed the bonfire, Grace appeared in front of me. 'Have you seen Emmi?' she said.

I shook my head.

Grace wrinkled her nose. 'I'm just a bit worried about her. She was really drunk and she went off with that mate of Flynn's from your college. D'you think she's all right?'

I raised my eyebrows. 'Emmi can look after herself.'

Unlike Leo.

I slipped off my heels and ran towards the house. Inside, I looked everywhere but I couldn't find him. Eventually I wandered outside again. It was well after midnight now, and most of the people from Norton Napier had gone. The bonfire had almost burned down to its embers, the flames dying inside it.

The air was freezing now, far colder than when I'd gone into the house to find Leo. I started to feel cross with him. He shouldn't have just assumed that I'd blabbed about him thinking he might be gay. Especially seeing as I hadn't. And I didn't expect him to thank me for chasing those guys away but storming off like that was totally over the top.

I passed a few patches of vomit. Yuck. Dad would be annoyed about that in the morning. I could see James and Grace sitting on the grass on the other side of the bonfire, a blanket around their shoulders. A couple, half-dressed, lurched out of some trees and staggered past me towards the house.

Music was still playing in the barn but not the dance stuff we'd had on before. Someone had put on a slow track.

Suddenly I forgot about Leo. Where was Flynn?

All I wanted right now was to hold him and dance in his arms. I smiled as the thought warmed my whole body.

'Flynn?' I yelled into the darkness. My breath misted faintly in front of me. I listened. No answering voice. Just the sound of crackling flames and distant music.

'Hey, River.' It was James, standing up, on the other side of the fire.

I raced over.

'He was here a second ago. He's just getting a cab for some of his mates.' James grinned. 'Cool party, eh?'

I smiled back. 'When he comes out, tell him I'll be down in the barn, yeah?'

James nodded and sat down again next to Grace. They were sipping cola, I noticed. I smiled to myself, wondering how much Grace's nervousness about James driving was reinforcing his parents' total ban on drinking.

I wandered down to the barn, my head full of a fantasy in which Flynn would arrive and we would dance together, alone.

The door was half open. I slid round it then stopped, unable to believe what I was seeing. Emmi and Stone were in the middle of the barn, slow-dancing together. Except that dancing hardly came into it. They were kissing furiously. Emmi was

182

practically falling out of her top, while Stone's hands . . . ew . . . were all over Emmi's bum.

For the second time tonight blind rage surged up from my gut.

'Emmi!' I yelled.

Stone jumped, letting go of her. Emmi stumbled a couple of steps backwards. She stared at me, her eyes all unfocused. Jeez, she was so off her head she could barely stand up.

I charged across the room and shut down the music. 'What the hell are you doing?' I shouted.

Emmi giggled. 'What does it look like?'

I glanced at Stone. He was glaring at me, his expression exactly caught between absolute embarrassment and total fury. I looked back at Emmi. 'He's not even fifteen yet,' I said.

'So?' Emmi giggled again. 'He's a better kisser than loads of guys half his age. No, I mean twice . . .' She giggled harder, then staggered sideways, holding out her arms for Stone to catch her. He grabbed her and hauled her upright. Then he turned to me.

'Go away,' he said.

I swore violently. 'Get away from her.'

'No.'

I wasn't sure why I was so angry. I mean, logically, Emmi was clearly far drunker than Stone was. And yet I felt protective towards him. He was my little brother. And Emmi was my age. Worse, I'd only ever seen her chew guys up and spit them out. Stone had no idea who he was dealing with.

'You can't go with her.' I marched towards him. 'It's wrong.'

'Why?' Emmi slurred.

'Yeah, why, Riv?' It was Flynn.

I turned round. He was standing in the barn doorway, smiling at me. His hair was ruffled and his T-shirt creased and dirty, and there was a black smudge across his cheek. For a second I was floored by how totally gorgeous he looked. Then I frowned. 'What d'you mean "why"? Stone's only fourteen. And Emmi's . . .'

'Emmi's Emmi,' Flynn said, walking towards me. 'And Stone's old enough to know what he's doing. Leave them alone. They're just kissing.'

I blinked furiously at him. Why couldn't he see that Stone was going to get hurt?

'She's already got off with one of the guys from college tonight,' I explained. 'She'll let Stone kiss her, then she'll just go onto someone else.'

'I'm still here, you know,' Emmi slurred.

Flynn laughed. 'What makes you think Stone wants anything more than that?'

I glanced at Stone. His face was bright red. But I could see in his eyes Flynn was right.

My mouth fell open.

'Having said that,' Flynn turned to Stone. 'You can't go any further, much as I understand you wanting to, mate. She's off her face. Look.'

We all stared at Emmi. She glared glassily back at us.

'I am so not my face off,' she said haughtily.

Flynn rolled his eyes, then looked at Stone again.

Without a word Stone turned and walked out of the barn.

Emmi staggered backwards until she reached one of the chairs in the corner of the room. She collapsed onto it, her long legs sprawling to the floor.

I turned on Flynn. 'I suppose you think that was helpful,' I said.

Flynn raised his eyebrows. 'Come on, Riv. How d'you think your brother feels? He turns up at this party fresh out of his first relationship, knowing all these older girls are going to be here. To his amazement, he pulls a total babe but, just as things are getting interesting, his sister appears yelling her head off that he's only fourteen. All I was doing was giving him a way out of the situation without feeling like a complete jerk.'

'All you were doing was interfering,' Emmi muttered.

I jumped. I had, momentarily, forgotten she was still in the barn.

Emmi stood up and advanced towards us. She stopped just a metre or so away, swaying slightly. Her face was screwed up in fury.

'You two are such awesome hypocrites. All loved-up for each other but nobody else can have any fun.' She poked her finger into my chest.

'Hey, Emmi.' Flynn pushed her arm away. 'Stop it.'

She spun round. 'You're worse than she is, you're so arrogant . . . yeah, you're so far up your own arse you can probably see your tonsils.'

'Emmi, that's enough,' I said.

Emmi swung a punch at Flynn. It missed by miles.

'For your information I wouldn't go with you, Flynn, if you were the last man on earth.'

'Good.' Flynn made a face at her. 'We're sorted then. Come on, Riv. Let's go insi—'

'I hate you both.' Emmi's voice rose even higher, so she was almost screaming. She sounded like a toddler having a tantrum, like her world was ending.

'Emmi, please.' I suddenly felt sorry for her. Maybe it wasn't just Stone who needed a way to save face. I reached out my hand. 'Come back inside with us.'

'No.' Emmi whipped her arm away, losing her balance again. 'Don't you *dare* start pretending to be nice, now,' she spat. 'You made out I was a total slag just then. But we both know that *you're* the slag.'

I stared at her. What the hell was she talking about?

'Emmi.' Flynn's voice was stern – a warning.

Emmi backed away from us. 'Slag. Slag. Slag.'

'Shut up,' Flynn snapped.

'Oh?' Emmi's eyes widened in mock-surprise. 'Hasn't River told you about Slug Tongue?'

19

All the air felt as if it was being sucked out of my body. How did Emmi know about the boy who kissed me? She'd been at the club, sure, but I hadn't told her about that revolting kiss – or that I'd nick-named the boy 'Slug Tongue'.

'What?' Flynn said.

'Tell him, River,' Emmi snarled. 'Tell him about the evening at the club. Tell him about Slug Tongue.'

Flynn looked at me. 'What is she talking about?'

I swallowed, trying to push down the panic that consumed me, trying to focus. 'It was a club we went to when . . . when you were in Ireland,' I said. 'There was this disgusting guy who tried it on. Nothing happened.'

Emmi snorted. 'You let him put his tongue in your mouth. You must have. How else would you know it felt like a slug?'

'He made me,' I said quickly. This wasn't quite

true, though I hadn't been expecting the kiss. I glanced at Flynn who was staring at me, horrified. 'What I mean is, he was this total idiot who lunged at me and it was so disgusting I felt sick . . .'

'Some guy tried to kiss you?' Flynn was staring at me, utterly appalled. 'Why didn't you tell me?'

'What for? It didn't mean anything to me . . . I ran *away* from him. And I didn't want to upset you.'

Flynn nodded, slowly. I could see him thinking it through in his head. 'So you stopped him?' he said.

'Yes.' I turned on Emmi again. How dare she try and hurt me like this?

'So *I'm* not the slag.' I spat. 'I'm not the one getting off with guy after guy and ending up with my best friend's brother.'

Emmi's eyes narrowed. And in that instant I knew she knew about James. A cold, sick panic clutched at my throat.

No. No. No.

'Just your boyfriend's best friend,' she said, suddenly sounding horribly sober.

My heart was beating hard against my ribs.

'River?' Flynn's voice was urgent. 'What's she talking about now?'

'Nothing,' I gasped.

'Nothing?' Emmi sneered at me. 'So when it's me, two guys a night is a slag. But when it's you, it's nothing?'

'River?' Flynn sounded half-strangled. 'What . . . ?'

I couldn't face him. I couldn't look round. I kept my eyes on Emmi, pleading with her not to say any more. To take what she had said back. To somehow make it all right.

And then Emmi turned to Flynn and I knew.

I knew that she was going to tell him. I knew that she'd been dying to find some way of upsetting him ever since he'd walked into the barn. And I knew, without a shadow of a doubt, that when Flynn heard he would hate me.

'Your best friend, Flynn,' she hissed. 'Think about it. He was at the club too.'

Flynn grabbed my shoulders. Spun me round. 'Look at me.'

I looked up. His eyes were dark gold in the dim glow of the barn lights. Hard as bullets.

'Is that true?' he said. 'You and . . . and James?'

My mind whirled as I tried to find a way of explaining that stupid, meaningless kiss to him. But the words stuck in my throat.

'Course it's true,' Emmi slurred.

'River?' Flynn's whole face was desperate. Pleading. 'What did James do? Did he try and kiss you too?' For a second he looked as if he was going to be sick.

'No.' I found my voice at last. 'It was nothing. *Nothing*. James was ... is ... totally into Grace. Always.'

'Then what's Emmi talking about?' Flynn stopped, his whole body rigid. I knew he could see in my face there was something I wasn't telling him. 'Was there a kiss or not?'

I gulped. 'No ... yes ... sort of ...'

'What?' Flynn backed away from me, his breath coming in heavy gasps. 'I can't believe James would do that.' He clenched his fists. 'I'm gonna freakin' tear him up ...'

He turned and raced out of the barn.

'No.' I pelted after him. 'Flynn. Stop.'

He was already flying past the dying bonfire. Into the house.

I ran after him, my breath burning in my chest. As I reached the house, Grace appeared outside the back door, a sleeping bag in her arms.

'Hi, Riv, did you find Em?'

'Where's James?' I grabbed her arm.

'What's the—?'

'Where the hell is James?'

'Getting our camping stuff out of the car. Why?'

I turned her round and started walking her past

the side of the house. 'You have to go back. Get in the car. Get James to drive away. It doesn't matter where. Just away from here.'

Grace was twisting round, trying to wrench herself out of my grip. 'What's the matter, River? You're frightening me.'

Emmi panted up behind us. She grabbed my shoulder. 'River, I'm so sorry.'

I ignored her.

'Grace,' I hissed. 'Flynn knows. He knows James and I had that stupid kiss and he's going to really hurt James if he finds him.'

Grace's eyes widened. She stood stock-still. 'Oh my God.' Her eyes flickered over to Emmi. 'You *told* him?' she breathed.

I stared at Grace. *Of course.* That's how Emmi knew.

'You told *her*?'

Grace's forehead wrinkled. 'She overheard something, Riv. That day we were talking about it while she was on the phone to Jean-Luc. She pestered and pestered me until I told her.' Grace turned to Emmi. 'You swore you wouldn't say anything.'

Emmi was crying now, her make-up running down her face.

'I'm sorry,' she mumbled incoherently. 'I'm sorry.'

Something in my head seemed to snap. 'Never

192

mind that now.' I gave Grace a push. 'I'll explain it to Flynn when he calms down. Get James. Get out of here.'

Grace gave me a final, terrified look. Then she turned and ran towards the front of the house. Emmi was still standing in front of me, weeping. In that instant I hated her.

'Get out of my house,' I said.

'River. Please, I'm sorry.'

'Just get out.'

She turned and stumbled after Grace. I waited for what seemed like an age. At last I heard the roar of the car engine and the crunch of the wheels on the small gravel drive.

I leaned back against the wall of the commune, breathing a sigh of relief. At least James was safe.

And then Flynn tore out of the back door. He stopped as he saw me. 'Was that James's car?' he hissed.

I nodded.

Flynn swore. He punched the wall with the side of his fist. 'I'll freakin' get him tomorrow,' he spat. 'I'll go down there and drag him out of wherever he hides his sorry—'

'It wasn't his fault.' The words blurted out of me. I couldn't let James take the blame like this. The last thing I wanted was to explain properly what I'd done but I couldn't stand by and watch Flynn and James's friendship fall apart over a lie.

'What are you talking about? You said he tried to kiss you.'

'No.' I shook my head. 'No. It wasn't like that.' I shivered. 'Look, Flynn, can't we go to bed and talk about it in the morning.'

I gazed up at him, hoping against hope that somehow we could curl up and hold each other and that he would calm down and that I could explain properly.

Flynn punched the wall again. 'No, we freakin' can't talk about it in the morning.' He glanced up at the house. The light was still on at the end of the first floor. Dad and Gemma's room.

'Come on.' He gripped me round the wrist and dragged me back down to the barn. Several of the lamps had gone out, leaving the building feeling darker and colder than before. Flynn swung me in front of him and crossed his arms. 'Tell me exactly what happened.'

20

I took a deep breath and told Flynn everything, starting with how upset I'd been when I saw the faked data on Facebook about him stealing iPads.

'I thought you'd been lying to me, that you didn't care about me anymore, so I went to this club with Emmi and Grace and James.' I went on, emphasising how much I'd drunk, both before and after arriving at the club. I told him how Slug Tongue had chatted me up and bought me yet more drinks – and how, when I realised what he was after, I'd run away from him.

I finally got to the part of my story where James and I had got into the minicab.

'So remember I was really drunk. And James was trying to be nice. Trying to look after me, like you'd have wanted him to. Once we were in the cab, I realised how totally out of it I was . . . how I should just shut up . . . but I couldn't stop myself from talking and . . . and I asked James if you were with anyone else.'

'Why would you have asked that?' Flynn demanded.

'Because when your Facebook account was hacked whoever did it put up that fake photoshopped picture of you with a girl, remember?'

'I remember,' Flynn said, his eyes boring into me. 'That was just a stupid, faked picture.'

'I know but . . . I was asking James whether you were with her and I hated myself for doing it . . . I thought he'd go straight and tell you. But I had to know. And when he said you weren't with anyone else I didn't believe him. And I got upset. And he was nice but embarrassed. And then I thought about that disgusting guy who'd tried to kiss me. And . . . and how it had made me feel sick. And I wanted . . .'

I stopped talking. Only one light was still burning in the barn now. I had no idea what time it was but I knew it was very late. I was tired, so tired. And way beyond cold. I hadn't been able to feel my feet for the last half an hour.

I looked up at Flynn. His forehead was screwed up in a frown.

'What did you want?' His voice was icy.

'I wanted to know . . . I know it sounds stupid but I wanted to know if it was always going to be like that. If kissing other guys was always going to make me feel sick . . .'

'So . . .?'

I gulped. 'So I asked James to kiss me.'

Flynn stood stock-still in front of me, his eyes on fire.

'And did he?'

'Not at first.' I blushed, remembering how I'd put my face right up to his, then put my lips on his. How I'd laughed. How the movement of my lips laughing had turned into a kiss. 'We just moved closer and it . . . it happened.'

Flynn's whole body shuddered. 'You kissed each other.'

'For about one second,' I pleaded. 'Then I remembered Grace and—'

'Grace?' Flynn took a step away from me. 'You remembered *Grace*?'

'She was *there* and I thought you'd stolen Alex's iPad and might be going out with that girl in the picture.' Tears welled up and squeezed out of my eyes. This was coming out all wrong. Fear gripped me around the throat.

'I thought you said you never doubted me.' Flynn took another step away. His eyes burned, his breathing was laboured. 'You said you trusted me.' He turned and paced across the barn floor.

'I did.' I was sobbing now, wringing my hands. 'I *do*. Please, Flynn, I love you. I was *drunk*. I'm sorry, I didn't know what I was doing.'

Flynn spun round. 'That's what my da said after every time he hit my mum. "*I'm sorry, I was drunk, I didn't know what I was doing.*"'

I stared at him, my whole body shivering.

'You know what else he said?' Flynn went on. 'That it would never happen again. But, guess what, it always did.'

'But that's different,' I said.

Flynn shook his head. 'I left everything to be here with you. I left my mum, my family, my school. For months I've put up with your dad patronising the crap out of me. With this stupid commune and all its stupid rules and its hippy-shit politics. All for you, River.'

'I thought you liked it here.' I stared at him. 'You never said you thought it was stupid.'

'I told you a million times,' Flynn spat. 'I called it the drop-out centre. Remember? But once I lived here, I bit my tongue about it, every day. Because you were here. And I didn't want to make it hard for you. Because I thought . . .' His voice cracked. 'I went to a new school. I went to those stupid anger management sessions. All of it total rubbish. I put up with that creep Leo. I even told him to tell me if anyone gave him a hard time, so I could stop him getting beaten up.'

I thought of the guys I'd seen earlier.

'And d'you know why I did all that? Even though I was dying to get Leo back for acting so loved-up around you all the time? Because of *you*. Because I couldn't bear the thought of you getting cross with me about it. Because I didn't want to upset you.' Flynn's face crumpled. He turned away from me.

I crept round to face him. Tears were welling up in his eyes. I reached up to touch his cheek.

'Please, Flynn,' I wept. 'It was a meaningless kiss. Grace knows – James told her – and *she* isn't angry.'

'It's different,' Flynn said flatly, pushing my hand away. 'James was honest. He didn't let her find out like this.'

'Yes, but . . . but I'd have told you too, except I knew you'd overreact and—'

'You think I'm overreacting?' A tear trickled down Flynn's cheek. He brushed it angrily away. I'd only ever seen him cry once before, after he'd beaten up his dad. My body twisted up inside.

'James was my best friend, River.' Flynn's voice cracked. 'My only real friend. And *you* . . .'

I tried to pull him towards me, but he stood there rigidly.

'I'm so, so sorry,' I whispered. 'Please let's go up to bed and curl up and hold each other. And . . .'

'I can't.' Flynn strode over to the nearest wall and leaned back against it. 'I can't . . .'

I walked over and leaned beside him. 'Please. We can—'

'Don't you understand?' Flynn's mouth trembled. 'I can't stop seeing you kissing him.' He thumped his forehead. 'It's in here, now.'

I shrank back against the wall. 'I love you,' I sobbed. I couldn't think what else to say. 'I love you. I love you.'

'You're a liar,' he said.

'Don't talk to her like that.' Leo's voice echoed round the room.

We both looked round. He was standing in the doorway, shaking, his white shirt completely covered in mud.

Flynn charged across the barn. 'Get out!' he yelled. 'This is none of your business.'

'No.' Leo's face was white with terror. 'I'm not going without River. Not unless I know she's safe.'

Flynn pushed him in the chest. Leo stumbled backwards. A new fear lurched inside me. Flynn would never hurt me but Leo was an easy target.

'I told you to get out,' Flynn shouted.

'Leo, I'm okay,' I said. 'Please go.'

'No.' Leo clenched his fists. 'Not if he's bullying you. I won't go without you . . .'

'Don't you dare talk about me like I'm not even here,' Flynn snarled. He turned to me. 'Been kissing him too, have you?'

'No, of course I haven't.'

'Leave her alone,' Leo yelled.

Thwack. With a sickening crunch Flynn's fist sank into Leo's jaw. Leo spun right round on himself and collapsed onto the ground. Flynn stood over him, fists clenched, panting.

I ran over. Leo knelt up, holding his mouth. Blood was pouring out from between his fingers.

I stared at Flynn. And in that moment I suddenly realised how little I'd understood him. Anger and a harsh, ruthless pride were in his bones. He was never going to change.

'Leo didn't hurt anyone,' I said, my whole body trembling.

Flynn just looked at me. For a second the fury in his eyes subsided and they shone a soft, agonised gold, full of longing and hurt and love. And then, as I watched, they hardened into cold pinpricks of a rage I couldn't begin to understand.

'Well, he's all yours now,' he said quietly. And then he turned and walked out of the barn.

I bent down over Leo. 'Are you all right?'

He stood up shakily. Blood was still pouring down his face. I put my arm round his waist. 'Come on, let's get you up to the house.'

We walked quickly up to the kitchen. I grabbed a tea towel and some ice and told Leo to press them against his mouth. Then I ran upstairs and knocked on Dad and Gemma's door.

Dad answered in his bathrobe. 'Hey, Riv, how's it going? Everything sounded quiet. I was just coming down to check . . .' He glanced at my dress. 'Hey, sweetheart, what's the matter? Is that *blood*?'

'There was a fight.' I caught my breath, unable to say Flynn's name. 'Leo's been hurt.'

I turned away to go back to Leo. As I glanced at our room, I wondered where Flynn was. There was no sound from inside and no light seeping under the door.

Dad and Gemma followed me down the stairs. Dad whistled when he saw Leo, while Gemma fetched the first-aid box from one of the kitchen cupboards. Dad tried to see inside Leo's mouth but there was too much blood.

'Leo's dad came in at about one, I think, River,' Dad said. 'Would you fetch him, please?'

I raced up to Leo's apartment. The commune felt eerily still now the party was over. I still couldn't see Flynn anywhere. Where was he?

Leo's dad was fast asleep. It took me a full minute of banging on his apartment door to wake him, then he stumbled after me to the kitchen. Leo was still sitting at the table, white-faced, while Gemma dabbed at his face.

Leo's dad paled at the sight of all the blood.

'I'm fine, Dad,' Leo said quickly.

'I think he is but we're going to have to take him to casualty,' Gemma said. 'He needs to be properly examined. He might need a stitch or something.'

'Who hit you?' Leo's dad asked, reaching for his son's arm.

It struck me that this was the first time I'd ever seen them touch.

Leo shook his head. He kept his gaze on the floor.

'For Pete's sake,' his dad said.

Gemma rested her hand on his shoulder. 'Hospital first, questions later,' she said.

A minute later Gemma and Leo's dad took Leo off in the car. Dad looked at me curiously. 'Are you all right, River?'

I nodded. Surely enough time had passed now for Flynn to have calmed down a bit. Maybe if I tried to explain again . . .

'I'm fine, Dad, just a bit wired. I'll be up in a second.'

'Okay.' Dad gave me a hug and padded off to bed.

I called Flynn's mobile. It was switched off, so I began searching the house for him. I was sure he wasn't outside anywhere. I'd been so close to the kitchen door while Gemma was examining Leo that I'd have heard if he'd gone out to the barn or the meadow again.

But Flynn wasn't in the house. I looked in our flat, then in all the communal rooms. I found a couple of partygoers asleep in the downstairs office and Stone snoring loudly on the living room couch but the rest of the communal rooms were empty.

I went back to our room and sat on the mattress.

And that's when I realised. Flynn's drawer – the middle one in the chest of drawers – was half open. I was sure it hadn't been left like that earlier. My heart was in my mouth as I stumbled across the room to look inside. The drawer was empty.

I darted across the room to the big trunk in the corner where we put our bags and school books. Flynn's bag was gone. Terrified now, I raced over to the hanging rail. My clothes were draped across it, though not in the same way they had been earlier. I tore them down. Empty hangers clattered to the floor. I looked around and gasped. Flynn's football boots and running shoes and other bits and pieces – all the things most useful or important to him – were no longer here.

I staggered over to the bed, unable to take it in.

He can't be gone. He can't. He must be here some-where. He's just angry. Trying to scare me. I sank onto the bed. *He's coming back. He's coming back.*

I sat on the covers, hunched over my knees. I caught sight of the framed photo he had given me earlier. It was on the other side of the bed from where I'd left it, face down, as if someone had kicked it over the bed. I picked it up. Miraculously the glass was still intact, though a little of the frame had been chipped away.

I placed the photo back beside the bed where it had originally stood.

Any minute he'll walk back in. Any second.

I didn't want to be asleep when he came back, so I sat up against the cold, hard wall, still in my clothes.

Waiting.

21

I woke with a jolt. It was still dark but I hadn't drawn the curtains last night and the sky was lighter than when I'd fallen asleep.

I twisted round so quickly I almost cricked my neck.

No Flynn.

I lay still for a moment, my body tensing as I remembered everything that had happened last night. I was on top of the covers, slumped sideways across the bed. Freezing cold.

I got up and found my phone. No texts or missed calls. I called Flynn but his mobile was still switched off, with no option to leave a message. I sent a text saying to *please, please call me*. I took the phone to the bathroom but he didn't call back. I had a pee, then a drink of water, then padded back to bed.

The whole house was silent.

I got under the covers, feeling strangely numb. I put the phone by the bed.

He's here somewhere. He's just punishing you. He'll be back.

It took me ages to warm up and even longer to fall asleep again.

I woke up slowly this time. Light was pouring in through the window. I could feel the warmth of it on my eyelids. I lay there for a second feeling happy. I imagined opening my eyes, seeing Flynn's face on the pillow beside me, feeling his hand stroking my cheek.

And then I remembered.

My eyes snapped open. The pillow next to mine was empty.

There was a soft tapping on the door.

'River?'

The tapping got slightly louder, then Leo's head poked round the door. I gasped at the sight of his face. The area round the left side of his lip was swollen and bruised. Even from the bed I could see where the lip was cut.

'Are you all right?' Leo tiptoed over. He was dressed in jeans and a jumper. His face was even paler than usual and there were dark rings under his eyes.

I stared at him. *No. I'm not all right.*

Leo got within a metre or so of the mattress, then stopped. He shuffled awkwardly from side to side. 'I'm fine. Just a cut lip,' he muttered. 'I was . . . I was so worried about you. I knew you wouldn't want me to say anything about Flynn. I told Dad it was some guys I didn't know who'd crashed the party . . .'

My eyes filled with tears as I remembered Flynn's face after he'd punched Leo. Then all the blood. I looked down at the stain on my dress. I looked up. Leo was staring at the blood too. He caught my eye and blushed.

'Sorry for bleeding all over you.' He touched his swollen lip. 'Has Flynn gone?'

I nodded again. Then I turned my face away, not wanting Leo to see me cry.

I could hear him padding back across the room and pulling open the door. It creaked. 'Er . . . I'm going to tell your dad you're awake,' he said hesitantly. 'I know he's worried about you seeing me beaten up.'

He left, shutting the door behind him.

I lay on my back, pulling the covers up around my neck. I stared up at the ceiling. Beaten up. Was that what Flynn had done to Leo? My heart told me it was. That punching him had been entirely unprovoked.

A few minutes later Dad came in. He sat down on the edge of the mattress. 'River? Are you okay?'

I nodded, not meeting his eyes.

'What happened last night? Leo told me some of it but there's stuff he's keeping back. Stuff to do with you, I think.' He looked round the room. 'And where's Flynn?'

I shrugged.

Out of the corner of my eye I could see Dad frowning. 'River, please, I'm worried about you. Did something happen to Flynn? Was he involved in this incident with Leo? Where is he?'

I shrugged again. *He's coming back. He's coming back.*

Dad sighed. The floor creaked as he stood up. 'I'll be back in a bit.'

He left. I lay there for a few more minutes, wondering where Flynn was. The fact that he'd taken most of his possessions suggested he had left the commune, at least for a while. I tried to work out where he could have gone with no money in the middle of the night. What would have been open? Who would have taken him in? Maybe one of his football buddies? My heart ached as I imagined him alone and trudging down the road towards Norton, where our college was. It was over two miles away. He could have got too cold to walk. Or twisted his ankle. Or been attacked by some gang.

I scrambled out of bed and found my phone. There were still no messages. No missed calls. I dialled his number but, as before, it was switched off with no option to leave a voice message so I texted him again, my hands shaking.

R U ok? Please come back. I love you. Please.

I sank back on the bed, praying Flynn was okay, praying he was on his way home right now. I curled up, hugging my arms round my chest. It still didn't feel real. Flynn was going to walk in any minute. Even if he thought I'd wanted to kiss James, he must have realised by now that it was a stupid one-off. A mistake. And he'd made mistakes too.

Surely he'd be able to see that.

The door opened again. Dad walked in. This time Gemma was with him.

They came over to the bed and sat on either side of me. Now I was on top of the bed rather than in it, I could see Dad registering that I was still in my party clothes.

'Is that *your* blood, River?' His voice was hoarse.

I shook my head.

'Just Leo's?'

I nodded.

I could see Dad and Gemma exchanging glances. Then Dad leaned closer to me. 'Please, River. Please talk to us. We're desperately worried. You seemed

fine last night. I mean, shaken but . . . But now . . .
Did something else happen? Did somebody hurt
you?'

I lay still. Part of me wanted to explain but I knew
that once I said the words that Flynn had gone, it
would make it real.

Dad leaned even closer. He shook my shoulder.
'River, please tell me what happened.' He shook me
harder. I curled up tighter into a ball. 'River.'

'No.' I sensed Gemma pulling him away.
'Sweetheart, listen.' Their footsteps echoed out to
the corridor. I could hear them whispering, though
not what they were saying. Then Gemma came
back in. 'I'm going to run you a bath, River, okay?
I'll help you.'

She left and a minute later I could hear the hot
water tank gurgling into action.

My phone beeped. I was across the bed and picking it up in a single movement. It wasn't Flynn. The
text was from Grace, asking if I was all right.

Two minutes later it rang. Emmi. I switched off
the call. She rang again. I switched off again. Then
she sent a text.

Am so so sorry please call me

I deleted the text.

Gemma came back in with a big bathrobe in her
arms. 'Let's get you undressed, okay?'

I stood up and let her unzip my dress. Her fingers moved swiftly and gently. As she slid the dress over my shoulders, I could see her searching my body, as if she was looking for something.

Then she stood back. 'You do your underwear, River.'

Obediently I unhooked my bra and peeled my knickers down my leg. Gemma covered me with the bath robe and tied it round me. Then she held my shoulders and looked into my eyes. There was such worry and such kindness in her expression that I wanted to cry again. Except that now the part of me that wanted to cry was buried deep inside me and I knew the tears wouldn't come. I stared dully back at her.

'River?' She hesitated. 'You don't have to talk. Just nod for yes. Shake for no. Okay?'

I nodded. I didn't want to shut myself off from Gemma. I just didn't want to speak. Couldn't speak.

'Last night, did anyone hit you?'

I shook my head.

Gemma took a deep breath. 'Did anyone . . . did someone force you to have sex or anything like that?'

I shook my head again.

'So . . . so . . . River, it's really important you are honest about this.' Gemma's voice shook. 'Did anyone touch you or do anything to hurt you at all?'

I shook my head a third time.

Gemma nodded. 'Okay, okay,' she said soothingly. 'Then let's get you into that bath.'

She took me through to the bathroom and sat there while I got in and soaked in the water. When I got out she wrapped me in the bathrobe again and we came into the bedroom. She found me some pyjamas and I got back into bed.

I knew at once somebody had been in the room while I was having my bath. The chest of drawers top drawer was shut. And my phone was in a different place by the bed. Dad, I was guessing, trying to work out what had happened.

I picked up my phone. Another text each from Grace and Emmi. Nothing from Flynn. I put it down and crawled under the covers. I felt exhausted. Like it was too much energy to even keep my eyes open.

I lay curled up again, the mobile in my hand, willing myself to sleep. If I could sleep then more time would pass and maybe when I woke up Flynn would be back, or be on the phone, calling me.

This time my sleep was disturbed and full of nightmares. I was in a dark house exploring its shadowy corners, the metallic taste of fear in my mouth all the time. I woke feeling more tired than ever. The sun was still bright, but lower in the sky, sinking down to the horizon. I got out of bed and went to the window. How often had Flynn and I stood here, arms around each other, just looking out like this.

I suddenly missed him like a part of my own body. I wished I hadn't had that bath earlier. It had washed away the last time he'd held me and touched me. And it had made the outside of me clean. Which didn't match the inside, all loathsome and dirty. I could see that now. Of course Flynn was right to be angry about me kissing James. It was a double betrayal. It was the same as if he'd kissed Emmi.

I closed my eyes as the thought of Flynn and Emmi filled me with a terrible jealousy that ate at my very soul. But Flynn hadn't done that. He didn't want Emmi. He wanted me.

I clung to that thought. He loved me. I was sure he did. Which meant he couldn't stay away from me. No more than I could stay away from him.

He's coming back. He's coming back.

22

I went back to bed. I took the photograph that Flynn had given me and hugged it to my chest, then I pulled the pillow that Flynn slept on across the bed and rested my head against it. It smelled of him. A mix of fresh sweat and my hair wax he was always borrowing and his particular smell: male and sharp and clean.

I lay there, hugging the pillow and the picture, until the light faded from the sky and the room went dark.

Gemma brought me a tray of food which I didn't touch. Then, later, Dad came back. He sat down next to the mattress.

'I've spoken to Grace and to Emmi,' he said. 'I'm sorry but I took their numbers from your phone while you were in the bath.'

Whatever. I shrugged.

'Anyway,' Dad went on. 'They've told me what happened last night.'

Oh God.

'They both wanted to come and see you but I told them it wasn't a good idea – not just yet.'

I nodded. I couldn't face either of them.

Dad gave a heavy sigh. 'And I've confronted Leo with what they both told me and he's told me the truth now so I think I understand what happened last night.' He paused. 'Obviously, despite him attacking Leo, we're all worried about Flynn. He isn't answering his phone, so I've rung around the local hospitals . . .'

My heart lurched.

'. . . and there's no sign that he's been anywhere near them. So I've called his mum and told her what's happened. I'm hoping that if anyone can get through to him it's her.'

I lay still. Inside, my stomach was churning. Now all those people knew I'd kissed James. I felt stupid and humiliated.

'And I called your mum too.'

I covered my face with my hands.

'River, I had to. She's terribly worried about you. I persuaded her that she couldn't do any good coming here tonight but I'm pretty sure she's going to drive up tomorrow. And if you don't eat something or talk to us then I'm going to call a doctor too.'

I turned away. Let him call who he liked. Let anyone who wanted traipse in here. They could come into my room. They could sit at the end of my bed. But they couldn't reach me.

Gemma came in later with more food, which I also didn't touch. When she came later to collect the tray I pretended to be asleep.

But I didn't sleep. I didn't sleep all night. Flynn's phone was still not taking voice messages, so I sent text after text . . . ludicrously long ones in which I tried to explain everything that had happened with James again, in which I told him over and over how much I loved him and how sorry I was that I'd hurt him.

After a while, the texts stopped going through. I rang again, to discover the number had been discontinued. I tried to find Flynn on Facebook but his account had been deleted. I went back to my phone and sat, staring down at Flynn's picture on my screensaver.

It felt like my last link with him had been cut. I fingered the heart on the silver chain around my wrist. I was numb, as if my life had been suspended.

I fell asleep at dawn and slept restlessly for a few hours. When I woke up Dad was in my room again.

'River?'

From the tone of his voice I knew something had happened. I sat bolt upright, my heart pounding.

'Flynn's mum just called me.' Dad reached out and took my hand. 'She's spoken to Flynn.'

He's all right. He's all right. I felt faint as the relief of it washed over me.

'But . . .' Dad hesitated. 'She doesn't know where he is. He wouldn't tell her but he's definitely not anywhere near here – and he's not back in London either. He told her he was okay . . . that he'd found somewhere to stay.' He hesitated again.

Did he say anything about me?

'He said that he wasn't coming back to the commune. He was adamant about it apparently. He didn't mention you but he's not coming back to live here, or going back to the sixth form college.'

I lay still, my face like stone. Inside I was empty. I couldn't accept what Dad had said. It couldn't be true.

The doorbell rang.

Dad raised his eyes. 'That'll be your mum.' He left the room.

I lay still, unable to move. I could hear raised voices downstairs. Then a door slamming. Silence.

The shock of what I'd heard ebbed and flowed through me, settling like washed-up rubbish on the shores of my mind.

Flynn wasn't coming back.

He didn't want me.

I was on my own.

As the truth of it sank in, I felt myself disintegrating. I was broken pieces, like the smashed mirror Flynn had replaced with our photo. I was splinters of myself, seeping away from my centre, sliding into the air around me.

I was nothing without him.

I didn't even feel afraid anymore. I was nothing definite enough to feel any emotion.

When Mum walked in I was so shut down I was barely even breathing.

She came straight over to the bed and leaned right across me. 'River?' she said, her voice all anxious and angry. 'River? This has to stop now. Please, darling. You're worrying everyone to death.'

Not Flynn. He's not worried. He's not even here.

I stared up, into her face. It felt like I couldn't have moved a muscle if I'd wanted to.

'Come on, River.' Mum grabbed my arm and shook it. Her voice rose. 'Get up. Now. Can't you see how selfish and stupid this is?'

'Hey,' Dad called out from the door.

Mum stood up and turned towards him.

'This is *your* fault,' she hissed. 'You let that criminal boy stay here. *In the same room*, for God's sake. I hold you entirely responsible for what's happened.'

Somewhere, a part of me knew that what she was

saying was unfair. I could hear Dad defending himself: calm but steely. And Gemma, anxious and soothing, trying to get them both to stop talking in front of me. But Mum had lost it.

'What the hell did you think would happen once the relationship was over? She's seventeen. *Just* seventeen. She doesn't have the resources to deal with this. That's so typical of you – not thinking through the consequences of your decisions.'

There was a short pause. Then Dad spoke.

'You're right. It was a mistake.' He sighed. 'But it's done now and knowing all that doesn't help River, does it?'

Mum didn't seem to know what to say to that. A few moments later they all trooped downstairs. Every now and then I could hear arguing voices, then it all went quiet. I got up and went to the loo. I felt giddy and had to lean against the wall as I walked. I guessed it was from not having eaten since Saturday night. It must be Monday morning now but I still couldn't face the idea of food.

When I came back to my room Leo was standing outside. We looked at each other. The swelling around his mouth had gone down but the bruising looked worse – an ugly, dark purple. I tried to smile at him but my mouth muscles didn't seem to want to move.

I went inside. He followed me, leaning against the wall as I got into bed and curled up again.

'It's World War Three down there,' he said. 'Your mum wants you carted off to the loony bin. Your dad wants to call some counsellor at Gemma's therapy centre and talk to her about what to do. And my dad keeps butting in, saying how the most important thing is that I give a statement to the police so that they can issue a warrant for Flynn's arrest.'

I looked up. Flynn had been arrested before, after he'd attacked his da. He'd been let off with a warning or something then but I imagined the police wouldn't go so easy on him a second time.

Leo shot me a rueful smile. 'I'm sorry I had to say it was him who hit me but your dad had guessed anyway from talking to Grace and Emmi. And you don't need to worry. I've already told my dad a million times I'm not talking to the police.' He paused. 'Not because I care about Flynn. But because you were there, which would mean you'd have to talk to them too. And I can see you don't want to talk to anyone.'

I kept looking at him. Somehow Leo saying that got through to me, in a way that nobody else's words so far had. He was telling it like it was, listening to me.

You don't want to talk to anyone.

He grinned. 'I actually came up to show you this.' He pulled a slim, wrapped package out of his pocket. 'I found it in the barn. Your dad and I were taking the sound system apart, ready for James's brother to pick up. I thought I'd bring this up to see if you knew who left it there. Looks like a book.'

He held the package out to me. I sat up, staring at it.

It *was* a book. It was the book of poems I'd bought Flynn as an anniversary present. *Rapture*, a collection of love poems by Carol Ann Duffy. They were on Flynn's syllabus for next term but that, of course, wasn't the only reason I'd decided to give them to him.

'Is it yours?' Leo asked.

I nodded.

'A present for someone?'

I looked at him.

'Him?'

I nodded again.

Leo's face hardened. 'Do you mind if I open it?'

I blinked. I did mind. And, then again, I didn't. What did it matter if Leo knew what I'd been planning on giving Flynn? What did anything matter now?

I shrugged, then lay back and closed my eyes.

Across the room I could hear the sound of tearing

paper. Then Leo whistled. 'Man, this is ace. I love her stuff.'

The sound of pages turning. Silence. Then footsteps across the room, towards me. The floorboards creaked. I could just picture Leo walking towards the bed. I felt his weight pressing down on one side of the mattress, then the air breeze past my face as he laid the book on the pillow beside me.

'Well, if it's yours I'll leave it here.'

I opened my eyes. Leo was staring down at the poems. He started to move away but I took his hand and placed it onto the book.

He glanced at me. 'You want me to have it?'

I shook my head.

'You want me to read the poems out to you?'

I nodded.

Leo considered me for a moment. Then he picked up the book. 'Okay.'

He started at the beginning and read the first poem, 'You'. It was this poem that had caught my eye and made me think of Flynn.

As Leo read, the misery that I'd been bottling up for so long started seeping out of me in scalding tears that trickled down my cheeks and that I made no attempt to brush away. Leo must have seen me crying but he made no comment and didn't stop reading.

He finished 'You', turned the page and read the next poem. Then the next. In the end he read solidly for about twenty minutes. His voice wasn't deep and expressive like Flynn's but it was melodic and sensitive – and he understood the poems. I was certain that even Flynn couldn't have read them with more feeling.

He stopped when Mum and Dad came in.

If they looked surprised to see him I couldn't tell, because I turned my face away as soon as I saw them.

'River, we need to make a decision. Your mum wants to take you home to *her* house right now. . .' Dad left the words hanging, presumably to see my response.

I shook my head. No way was I going back to Mum's. She had no idea how I was feeling – and no sympathy for me either. Anyway, I wanted to be here, waiting, in case Flynn changed his mind and came back.

'In that case,' Dad went on, 'we've agreed she will stay here for a couple of nights while we get the doctor in to see you.'

I turned away again.

I could hear shuffling by the door, then Mum and Dad left. I looked up at Leo, wondering what he was going to say. But he just picked up the poetry book and carried on reading.

He read all evening, only taking a break to bring up his supper on a tray. He offered me some. 'Why don't you have a roll? They've got honey on.'

I looked at him again. I knew Leo didn't even like honey. And I also knew that he knew I loved it. He was self-consciously avoiding my gaze, his eyes fixed on the book in front of him.

He started reading again but I wasn't listening. I was suddenly aware of just how hungry I was. How weak I felt. How every cell in my body was insisting that I reach over and take a roll. Without me being consciously aware I was doing it, my hand was on the plate, picking up the nearest roll. I bit into it, tasting the floury softness of the bread and the sticky sweetness of the honey. I'd never tasted anything so delicious in my life. I took another bite and another, now cramming the food in.

Leo reached over and took what remained of the roll out of my hand. He put it back on the plate and looked up.

'Take it easy,' he said, 'or you'll be sick.'

I nodded, knowing he was right. I could already feel the food working its way through me. Even those few little bites were filling me up. I sat back, as Leo tucked into his own roll. Every so often he would tear off a bit and offer it to me. Just a little bit at a time.

I ate it eagerly, wondering how he was managing to swallow the food, knowing how much he hated honey.

Soon all the rolls were gone. Leo picked up the plate and smiled.

'Your dad was wondering if it would help to see any of your friends. Grace, maybe?'

I shook my head. Friends would expect conversation – and I didn't have that to give. I took Leo's hand and squeezed it, trying to show with my eyes that he was enough. Leo smiled again and went downstairs. I slipped into a deep sleep almost straight away and didn't wake up until the following morning.

23

The doctor was a woman – youngish and friendly. She seemed nice but as soon as she started asking me questions I could feel myself closing up like I had around Mum and Dad.

Flynn was in my head, filling me up. There was no room for anything else. I forced myself to nod and shake my head to the doctor's questions.

No, I wasn't in any pain.

No, I wasn't having suicidal thoughts.

Yes, I was sure that at some point I would start talking again.

While the first two things were true, I didn't, in fact, feel confident that I would ever speak. The longer I went without doing so, the less point I could see in starting again.

I had everything I could possibly need. Food and shelter and Leo reading to me. That filled up the five per cent of me that wasn't consumed by Flynn. The rest of the time, with the rest of my being, I thought about him.

I was with him in my silence, reliving his presence, his voice, his laugh, his body – all the things we did and said, our lovemaking and our arguments, the way he looked at me. And all the time there was this gaping hole in my stomach, this numbness, where I contained the pain of missing him, of knowing that I had driven him away, of having to face the fact that he hated me, that I might never see him again.

After the doctor left, Mum and Dad and Gemma came in to see me. Dad explained that the doctor had recommended I was left to work through my feelings for a few more days. So long as I was eating and sleeping, then she thought it was better not to pressure me further into speaking.

'But we all agree that this can't continue for too much longer and that once you do feel able to talk, you'll see a therapist.'

I closed my eyes and turned away again.

No way was I talking to a stupid therapist.

I caught a whiff of Mum's perfume and looked up. She was standing over me, her arms folded. 'You should think yourself lucky you have people prepared to . . .' She caught her breath. 'I will stay on here, River, but I need to know if that's what you want.'

I looked into her eyes. The truth was I didn't want her here. I could see how angry she was, and, also, how hurt. For a few seconds I felt deeply, horribly guilty. But I couldn't have her here every day, fussing over me with all that barely repressed fury. I just couldn't.

I took her hand and squeezed it, then I shook my head.

No, Mum. I don't want you here.

She nodded briskly, then bent down, kissed my forehead and left.

Leo stayed home all that week. He brought me my breakfast every morning. Tea and toast, though now with jam on his bread instead of honey. We sat and ate together, then he read me the Carol Ann Duffy poems again.

Sometimes he translated them into Spanish or French as he read. I liked that, listening to the rhythm of the sounds, soothed by his voice. Sometimes he talked about them afterwards, saying what he thought they were about. Sometimes he'd finish a poem and read it again straight away, as if he was trying to make sense of it.

Often he'd pick up the book and choose a poem at

random. Except, after a while, I realised it wasn't random at all. He was choosing the ones that made me cry . . . the ones that made me think of Flynn.

One in particular he read over and over again.

I don't know how he knew that 'Row', with its raw, painful images, would help. I still hadn't cried properly over Flynn but when I heard that poem, so full of love and loss, my tears leaked out, easing the unbearable pressure of my feelings.

When Leo finished reading Carol Ann Duffy he brought in his MP3 player and played me music I'd never heard of – random stuff from ages ago, a total mix of sounds and styles.

'Do you want to hear the guy my mum named me after?' he asked one afternoon. 'He's called Leonard Cohen. Have you heard of him?'

I shook my head. Leo's full name was *Leonard*?

'Listen to this.'

Leo played track after track and I would shake or nod, to indicate if I liked it enough to hear it again.

Somehow, though he never wrote any of my choices down, he didn't forget what I liked.

Of course, I did know some of the music. Some of it I'd listened to with Flynn. I'd hear it again now, with Leo, and I would curl over, hiding my face, weeping again.

He let me cry. He never tried to make me talk. He

never tried to hold me. He just sat with me, letting me feel.

Bringing me back.

A week passed.

I slept very badly on the Saturday night, tossing and turning all night. I'd started worrying about Flynn again. About where he was and how he was.

And who he was with.

The thought of him with other girls consumed me with jealousy. Great, fierce waves of it that hurt so much I had to hold my breath against the pain, just waiting for it to pass. But the worst thing was the emptiness, that sense I had of being lost. An abandoned child, wailing into the darkness.

On Sunday I woke as the door opened, and turned eagerly, expecting it to be Leo. It was Dad.

I was shocked by how thin and grey he looked, his face drawn and old. He set down my breakfast tray and stroked the hair off my face. He didn't speak for a few minutes then, at last, he said: 'You know, you're going to have to face the world some-time, sweetheart.'

I could hardly bear the sadness in his voice and his eyes. I wanted to speak to him, to say I was sorry that I'd put him through so much pain. But I was so buried now under my layers of silence that I didn't know how.

'Leo would've brought up your tray,' Dad said, 'but his father's taken him out. They'll be home later and I expect he'll come up and see you then. You know he's going back to school tomorrow. That's going to be a big thing for him. I think he feels self-conscious about how he looks with that bruise on his face.'

I nodded, feeling guilty again. All this week Leo had spent time with me. *For* me. Listening to music and reading poems – even eating honey sandwiches. And, okay, he'd told me a bit more about his mum – how she'd been ill for several months before she died. How close they'd been. But everything he'd done had been about me. About helping me.

I hadn't given a moment's thought to how he might be feeling about . . . about anything.

I felt a stab of self-loathing.

I waited eagerly for him to come home. But it was dark before I heard the car pull up outside. I checked the time. It was after nine. I hoped Leo wouldn't think that was too late for him to come up.

I waited for what seemed like ages.

At last there was a soft rap on the door and Leo stuck his head round. He smiled, his eyes a sparkling blue, then came over and sat down beside me on the bed. He said nothing.

I picked up the book of Carol Ann Duffy poems and handed it to him.

He shook his head and put it down. I frowned. Didn't he want to read?

Then Leo cleared his throat. 'I had a good day with Dad today,' he said. 'The best we've had for . . . for ages.' He paused. 'And I was thinking about school. We're starting on *Jane Eyre* soon, remember?'

I nodded.

'I was thinking maybe I could read that to you, seeing as we've read all the Duffy poems about ten times each.'

A broad grin spread across my face. I nodded eagerly.

'Okay. But there's one condition.'

I raised my eyes.

'You have to ask me to do it.'

His words hung in the air between us. I stared at him. He was expecting me to speak?

Leo stood up and took a step away from the bed. 'You *can* speak, River, so I think you should. I mean, at first I understood, you were in shock or whatever. You needed to protect yourself. But now, you have to move on.'

I stared at him, suddenly furious. How dare he make demands, like . . . like everyone else? And

233

since when had he become so confident around me? Two weeks ago he hardly looked me in the eye.

Leo took another step away.

'Fine. I'll come by in a couple of days, see if you're ready to speak then. I just want you to ask me to read. It's only polite, really.'

My heart filled with fury.

Leo walked to the door.

I suddenly saw the next two days, stretching on like today had, only with no visit from Leo to look forward to at the end of them.

The fury transformed to fear.

Leo opened the door.

'Leo?' My voice came out in a croak. It felt weird, hearing myself speak out loud.

He turned round.

'Please read to me.' As I said the words, my voice somehow bridged the chasm between my body and my mind. I finally connected with the terrible pain, like a poison that crept through my veins, exploding inside every cell, worse than anything I'd ever known.

'Aaagh.' I curled up into a ball. It was more than I could bear. It would kill me. I wailed into my pillow. Deep, dark noises poured out of me, along with tears and spit and fury. My nose and eyes and mouth were streaming, my whole being focused in

234

my heart which was surely breaking and dying and drowning in the unbearable knowledge that Flynn had left me. And that he wasn't coming back.

I don't know how long I bawled like that but when I was too exhausted to do it any longer I looked up. Leo had gone. Dad was sitting there, his gentle eyes filled with tears. He held out his arms and I crawled into them, still sobbing.

'I know, sweetheart, I know.' He stroked my hair as I cried, incoherently wailing about Flynn and what had happened and how I couldn't live without him and how I couldn't bear feeling like this and how I wanted to die from the pain of it.

In the end my sobs subsided to shuddering gasps and I leaned my whole weight against Dad. He held me and rocked me to and fro like a baby, and as my tears finally dried, he whispered in my ear:

'This too shall pass. This too shall pass.'

24

That night I fell asleep with Dad holding my hand. I slept better than I had all week and woke feeling hungry – and lighter somehow. Someone had been in already and left me a cup of tea.

I felt a stab of guilt. Dad, Gemma and Leo had between them looked after me completely for the whole of the last week and I'd been too wrapped up in myself to even notice.

It was light and sunny outside, almost ten o'clock. I took a sip of my tea. It was cold. Maybe I'd go down to the kitchen and make myself another cup. I padded downstairs. I wasn't sure who would be around. Leo, I knew, would have gone back to school this morning. I kind of hoped I wouldn't bump into any of the other commune residents. Ros had come up to sit with me a few times but I hadn't seen the others all week.

I didn't want to face them. I didn't want to have to

talk to them. I know it sounds crazy but there were actually butterflies in my stomach as I walked along the corridor into the kitchen. It felt weird being outside my room.

Thankfully, the kitchen was empty. I made myself a cup of tea and some toast and sat down at the table. I drank the tea and nibbled on the toast. After a few mouthfuls, I didn't feel hungry any more and the food tasted like cardboard. I pushed it away. Then I got up and put the leftover toast into the recycling box. Dad and Gemma were always nagging me to eat more but I seemed to have completely lost my appetite. I didn't want one of them coming in and pestering me to finish the food.

As I straightened up, Gemma and Ros walked in.

'River?' Gemma beamed at me. 'How are you feeling?'

'Okay,' I lied. I tried to smile at her. 'Well . . . better.'

'Do you want some breakfast?' Gemma said.

'Had some.' I indicated the empty plate in my hand.

Ros plonked her bag on the kitchen table and started rifling through it. 'Pop the kettle on, then,' she said. 'I've got time for a cup before I go.'

Gemma rolled her eyes at me and moved towards the kettle.

'I'll do it,' I said.

I made tea and the three of us sat down at the table.

'Your dad's working out of the commune today,' Gemma said. 'But he's going to call in at lunchtime, see how you are.' She paused. 'He'll be so pleased you're up.'

'And talking,' Ros added.

'He's been so worried about you.'

I thought about how Dad had looked last night. I looked down at the table. 'I'm sorry.'

Gemma patted my hand. 'Hey, don't beat yourself up.'

'No. You can leave that to the men in your life,' Ros said sarcastically.

We all laughed. Then Gemma brought out some biscuits and we sat there for a bit. I didn't eat or say much. Ros did most of the talking. She said things were going well with Leo's dad, then told us about various guys she'd been with previously and how they'd cheated on her or walked out when she was at her most vulnerable.

I could see Gemma glancing at me, anxiously. But I didn't mind hearing about Ros's bad times. In a way it was flattering. She was talking to me like a friend her own age, as if now I'd been dumped by Flynn I was part of a club I hadn't known about before.

I kept thinking about him though, all the while she was talking. The way Ros told it she'd never put a foot wrong. But I had. I'd kissed Flynn's best friend.

I was scum.

After a while, Ros left for whatever work appointment it was she had. I told Gemma I was going to get dressed.

'You sure?' she said.

I nodded. 'Then I don't mind doing some chores. I'm kind of a week behind.'

Gemma grinned. 'Don't worry about that today. Why don't you get dressed while I do us some lunch. Maybe afterwards we could go outside. I bet you could do with some fresh air.'

So I got dressed. I cleared the room up too, putting the few things Flynn had left, and the photograph he had given me, in the box where we kept our school things. And I took a long, hard look in the mirror. I was thinner. Normally I'd have been delighted to have shed a few pounds but now all I could think was that my clothes were hanging off me, my hair was lank and straggly and my skin was grey. But the worst thing was how dead my eyes looked.

I stared at myself. It didn't matter how I looked. And dead was how I felt.

I went back downstairs and ate almost half the bowl of soup Gemma put in front of me for lunch. Afterwards, I went outside. I avoided the barn, walking instead across the field, past the charred remains of the bonfire, to the apple orchard where I'd found Leo being bullied on the night of the party.

It was hard to face those reminders of that terrible night but I knew I had to. The desperation on Dad's face last night plus the look of anxiety on Gemma's today told me I had to start pretending that I felt better . . . to at least look as if I was coping.

After about ten minutes wandering about in the chilly sunshine, I felt exhausted. I went up to my room and slept for an hour.

I hadn't been awake long when Leo came back from school. He came and sat at the end of the mattress as usual, and started telling me what had happened at school. Apparently Flynn dumping me, punching him and running away was the talk of the college.

'Kirsty asked how you were,' he said.

I nodded. Kirsty was still pretty much my closest friend at Norton Napier. She'd got off with some guy at the party and left early. She'd texted me a couple of times in the week. I hadn't texted back. I had the nagging sense, from her message, that she was really more interested in getting all the gossip than in how I was – but maybe that wasn't fair.

I started thinking about Emmi and Grace. At first, after last Saturday, I'd been too angry to imagine ever talking to them again. But since then I'd changed. I was still certain I would never speak to Emmi but Grace hadn't really done anything wrong. Okay, so she'd told Emmi a secret but only because Emmi had half overheard it anyway. That was hardly Grace's fault. And I knew how difficult it was for Grace to lie and how pushy and persuasive Emmi could be.

Grace had called me every day this week. Unlike Kirsty, I was sure she really did care how I was. Maybe I should ring her later . . .

'So do you want me to do that?' Leo's voice brought me out of my thoughts.

'Sorry, do what?'

'I was just saying Ms Ransome gave me some work for you to do at home. There's a couple of essays and some *Jane Eyre* reading.' He hesitated. 'D'you still want me to read it to you?'

I frowned. It struck me that Leo hadn't actually looked me in the eye since he'd walked into the room. My heart sank. It had been so easy between us, last week, when I hadn't been talking.

'I'd love you to read,' I said, with as much feeling as I could.

He looked at me at last, his pale blue eyes shy and questioning.

'How was today?' I said.

He shrugged. 'Okay, I guess. At least...' He stopped.

'At least what?'

'Nothing.' He looked down.

'Hey.' I reached over and prodded his chest. 'I thought we were friends?'

Leo looked up.

'So spill. What happened?'

'I just... I meant that it was a quiet day. No one... you know, no one hassled me.'

I suddenly remembered how close Leo had come to being beaten up by those guys in the trees at the party. My whole body flooded with shame that I'd forgotten – and that Leo must think they only knew he was gay because I'd spread the information at school.

'Leo, I never told anyone what you told me... about... you know... What those guys in the orchard—'

'Don't.' Leo held up his hand, his face bright red. 'I know you didn't say anything.'

I frowned. 'But those guys...'

'. . . thought I was gay? Yeah, I know.'

'But how . . . ?'

Leo took in a deep breath. His chest heaved. 'They *assumed* I was gay, just like people did in my last school. Some of them in our class have been saying stuff since the first week, though up until the party it was just nasty comments and a bit of pushing me around. Those guys were different . . .' He tailed off.

I couldn't believe it. How come I'd never noticed Leo being taunted and bullied at school? Had I really been so wrapped up in Flynn that I hadn't seen? I knew most of the people in our class thought Leo was weird but, as far as I was aware, he'd been ignored, not picked on.

'I had no idea,' I gasped. 'Oh, Leo, I'm so sorry. Why didn't you say something before?'

'What would you have done?' He paused. 'If I'd told you, you'd have just asked Flynn to sort them out.'

I looked away. I wanted to deny what he said, but I knew it was true.

'Flynn asked me back in our first week if I was okay,' Leo said, his voice dull and flat. 'He offered to deal with anyone who had a go at me . . . but I told him to get lost.'

'But wouldn't his protection have been better than—'

243

'No.' Leo got up. 'Look, it's nothing personal, River, but I don't want to talk about this right now. I'll read to you later.' And he walked out.

I sat back, baffled. Leo had been so open last week. Why didn't he want to talk now?

25

I got up later and went downstairs for the evening meal with everyone at the commune. They all seemed pleased to see me. Ros gave me a hug while Leo's dad, John and the nerdy IT guy all said hello then carried on their animated conversation about the best place on the commune to use our home-grown leaf mould – with interjections from John's wife Julia on the state of the potatoes from the vegetable garden. I sat next to Leo and tried to eat my supper. Gemma had made vegetable lasagne, which was one of my favourites. I was sure she'd done it specially and I tried to eat more than a few mouthfuls, but once I'd had enough to stop feeling hungry, the food tasted like slime.

Dad talked to me after dinner. He said he was pleased I was up and eager to do chores. 'Focusing on physical and mental tasks will help give yo space while you work through your feelings said. 'Plus they'll give you balance: school tire out your mind and chores to tire out your body.'

I nodded, only half listening. I was wondering if Flynn had found a job, or somewhere permanent to stay. I was wondering if he was thinking about me. I was wondering if he had found someone else.

Dad and I agreed that I should go back to school in a couple of days. He also wanted me to see a counsellor. 'Gemma's found someone she thinks will be helpful at the therapy centre. You can start seeing her next week.'

I didn't want to do it. After witnessing Flynn's anger management session, I'd kind of lost faith in the whole idea of counselling and therapy. In the end I agreed, reluctantly – it seemed to mean so much to Dad and Gemma.

Later, Leo read the first few chapters of *Jane Eyre* to me. He seemed tense and awkward when I tried to talk to him afterwards and soon left, saying he was tired after going back to school.

I sat on my bed, feeling miserable. Dad and Gemma were great but I missed having a friend to talk to. So I called Grace.

when she heard my voice. Soon

ng. She kept saying she was

ng that had happened. I asked

ne up at the weekend – and not

The next day I helped Gemma prepare the evening meal. Then I did some of the schoolwork Leo had brought home for me. I wasn't looking forward to going back to college tomorrow and I wanted to be as prepared as possible. I didn't read any more of *Jane Eyre* though. I was hoping Leo would do that. After feeling miserable that he'd been so awkward last night, I'd realised just how important his friendship was to me.

'I've got a favour to ask you,' I said, when he got home that afternoon. 'Can I come up to your apartment?'

Leo's eyes widened in alarm. 'Sure.' He started running towards the stairs. 'Er . . . just give me five, yeah?'

I wasn't sure why he needed a head start but I waited five minutes then climbed the stairs and knocked on his apartment door.

He opened it, and stood back to let me in. I looked around, curious. I hadn't been inside Leo's flat since he and his dad moved in nearly six months ago. Well, there hadn't been any reason to. It was on the opposite side of the building from Dad's place and I'd spent all my time with Flynn. But now it seemed important to come here. If Leo and I were going to be friends, I wanted to see where he lived when he wasn't in the communal areas.

The flat's central living room was massive and bleak – a TV in the corner, two big sofas and a table with four chairs in the corner. There was no rug on the floor, no pictures on the walls, and no books or ornaments on the single empty shelf. It didn't look very different from when it had been empty.

'Where's your room?' I asked.

Leo led me to one of the rooms on the right. It was completely different than the living area, with virtually every centimetre of wall space covered with posters of the sea and printouts from websites and photos, most of which I was sure Leo had taken himself. The room itself was neat and much tidier than I was expecting. A single bed with a plain blue quilt cover and an old wooden wardrobe stood along one wall. At the end of the room was a long, low window with a padded seat. I crossed the room and sat down. I could see right across the fields, past the oak tree and down to the edge of the apple orchard.

I caught sight of the barn roof and looked away, a sick surge of misery bringing new tears to my eyes. I forced a smile onto my face. I'd done enough crying for a lifetime.

'This seat is so cool,' I said. 'You could sit and read here for hours.'

'I do.' Leo was smiling but underneath I could see he felt really awkward.

My heart sank. Why was this so difficult? I looked over at the photos and pictures closest to the bed. There were several of a pretty woman with delicate features like Leo's and the same soft, shy eyes.

'Is that your mum?' I asked.

Leo nodded. 'Dad threw out loads of stuff – he said it was too painful – but I saved some of her things.' He took a shoebox from under his bed and offered it to me. I took the lid off and peered inside.

There were more photos and a gold chain and a china teacup with a chip in the side. I lifted out a tube of hand cream. It was twisted and scrunched, almost empty. I opened the top and sniffed at the cream inside – a faint scent of lily of the valley.

'It's how she smelled,' Leo said.

I looked at him. 'Do you miss her?'

He met my gaze. 'Every day.'

I put the hand cream away and the lid back on the box. Leo placed it back under the bed and we sat in silence for a moment. Strangely, Leo seemed less awkward now. I knew it was special that he'd showed me that box – and I was glad that he had.

I glanced at the photos by his bed again. There were several of the oak tree and the apple orchard, and then a gap where it looked like a photo had been removed.

'What went there?' I asked.

Leo shrugged. 'Nothing.' He paused. 'What did you want to ask me?'

I smiled. 'I just wanted to ask you if you'd have lunch with me tomorrow in the cafeteria at school. I'm just feeling weird about going back. I mean, I know it sounds a bit pathetic but . . .'

'I'd love to.'

Leo's face creased with such obvious relief that I laughed. 'Jeez, what did you think I was going to ask you?' I said.

He mumbled something incoherent and blushed again.

I rolled my eyes. 'Look, Leo. I really like you. I don't care if Flynn didn't. And if you don't want to be friends that's fine but I'd rather you told me to back off, instead of one minute making out like you want to talk, and then going all weird on me the next. If we're friends you should be able to tell me what the problem is. I mean, I don't care if you're gay or straight or whatever, I just want to hang out with you.'

Leo stared at me. 'I'm not gay.'

'Really?' I frowned, feeling confused. Hadn't Leo more or less *told* me he was gay? Wasn't that why those stupid guys wanted to beat him up? 'But before you said . . . I don't understand.'

Leo leaned forward, his head in his hands. 'I did

wonder if I might be gay a while ago. Not because I liked boys. But because I didn't really like girls. Not like other guys did. And then, well, then I realised I *did* like girls. A lot. At least, some girls.' He looked up. 'Sorry, I know it doesn't make sense. You'll probably hate me now for being stupid . . .'

'I don't hate you.' I sat back in the window seat, hugging my knees. 'What made you know for sure that you liked girls?'

Leo gave me a long, miserable look. 'You,' he said.

26

'Me?' I could feel my cheeks getting hot. Was Leo saying he *liked me*? I'd had suspicions months ago – as had Flynn – but I'd totally put them out of my head.

Leo nodded, his own face now reddening. 'It's kind of ironic,' he said. 'For years I was bullied because I like reading and poems and I'm not into stupid team games where the point is for one set of macho jerks to beat up another set and I'd started to think maybe I actually was gay, like they said, and . . . and then I got here and I knew for sure that I wasn't but I couldn't say anything.' He paused. 'I actually told you I thought I might be gay so that you wouldn't stop being friends with me. How screwed up is that?'

I bit my lip. What on earth did I do now? The last thing I wanted was to hurt Leo's feelings but I couldn't let him think that just because Flynn had gone there was any chance of us getting together.

'I didn't realise,' I stammered.

'Flynn did.' Leo's voice hardened as he spoke.

There was an awkward pause.

'What do you mean?' I asked.

'Flynn saw . . . how I felt . . . and he made it clear I had to keep my distance.'

'He *said* that?'

'No, not exactly.' Leo sighed. 'But he still made it obvious. That's why I kept away from you all summer.' He hesitated. 'I think that's why he hit me too.'

'No,' I said, my head spinning. 'No, he was just mad at me.' The memory of the evening Flynn had been in a bad mood after counselling flashed into my head. He had asked me then if anyone else had ever tried it on. I closed my eyes, remembering how I'd lied and told him I'd never kissed any other boy.

'Was that why you were so angry when I got rid of those guys at the party?' I asked. 'Was that about Flynn too?'

'That was the most humiliating moment of my life,' Leo said, his voice barely a whisper. 'Think about it . . . *me* being rescued by *you* because of *him*. I couldn't bear what you'd think of me. How pathetic you must think I was.'

'I don't think you're pathetic. I think you're . . . great. You couldn't help those guys picking on you.

I'm the one who screwed up that night.'

'No, you didn't do anything wrong. Flynn had no right to be mad at you.'

'Yes, I—'

'*No*,' Leo interrupted. 'I heard that whole story about you getting drunk at the party months ago and asking James for a stupid kiss. It was nothing . . . nothing that any sane person would have minded.'

My stomach knotted. Leo was saying Flynn had overreacted . . . that I wasn't guilty of betraying him. But I had. I'd kissed his best friend and I'd lied about it.

'*Nothing* Flynn did was right,' Leo went on bitterly. 'I hated the way he swaggered around all the time, doing his tough guy thing, making out he was better than everyone else. And the way he'd look at you – like he owned you – I hated that.'

I stood up. I couldn't stay here and listen to Leo saying these horrible things.

'You didn't know him,' I said. 'You didn't understand him, nobody did.'

'Right.' Leo pressed his lips together into a thin, angry line.

I took a step to the door.

'So does that mean you don't want to be friends anymore?'

It sounded so childish, the way he said it, that I almost smiled.

I turned and faced him as I reached the door. I wasn't prepared to listen to Leo dissing Flynn like he was vermin but I wasn't ditching my only real friend over it. 'We're mates,' I said. 'That's that.'

The next morning, Leo and I took the bus to college together. Dad had offered us a lift but Leo wasn't bothered and I wanted to keep everything as low-key as possible. I was dreading being back at Norton Napier and my arrival was as bad as I'd expected. People pointed and whispered as Leo and I walked along the corridor. Later, in class, was just as awful. Everyone acted really weird around me, even Kirsty. It was like I had some terrible disease they were scared of catching. None of them suggested meeting up after school. And when they asked me questions about what had happened I didn't feel they cared about me – they just wanted information.

Lunchtime came and I found Leo at a table on his own in the cafeteria.

'I feel like a leper,' he said. 'You know, something untouchable. Everyone's still staring at my face. How about you?'

'Leprosy would be a breeze after this,' I muttered.

I'd decided the fairest thing I could do with Leo was be all jokey and matey. There was no point talking about his feelings for me. And I certainly wasn't going to talk about Flynn with him anymore.

I looked around the canteen at the various counters. Flynn had come up behind me so often as I queued at them, grabbing me from behind and pulling me into a kiss, not caring who saw or what they thought. I felt a sudden stab of misery. How was I going to get through the rest of my life without him?

After a few days, college life settled down. Leo's bruise finally faded away and people stopped staring at me as I passed but I still felt there was a huge distance between me and everyone else at Norton Napier.

I looked forward to seeing Grace at the weekend. She and James were planning to drive up for the whole of Saturday and I imagined that hooking up with old friends, even ones as involved with my past with Flynn as Grace and James, would be just what I needed.

It wasn't.

Both James and Grace seemed awkward around me, right from the start. I knew that James hadn't seen or heard from Flynn since the night of the party and I wondered at first if he blamed me for what had happened. But as our time together went on, I realised that far from being resentful towards me, James was furious with Flynn.

'He *totally* blew the whole thing out of proportion,' he said. 'Running off in the middle of the night and leaving you in that state.'

'But . . . but he thought we'd betrayed him,' I said.

James shook his head. 'You made a tiny mistake, River. *Way* tinier than most of the mistakes Flynn's ever made but he was only seeing it from his point of view. It was really selfish.'

I tried to explain that Flynn had resented other stuff too – his life at the commune and his counselling sessions – but James didn't want to hear it. I gave up completely when Grace started hinting that maybe I'd soon be ready to make up with Emmi. As far as I was concerned, I never wanted to set eyes on her again.

Grace and James left early, after a few hours, and I felt relieved. It wasn't just that we saw my fight with Flynn differently . . . In the past couple of weeks I'd been in a place Grace didn't know existed. She had no understanding of what I'd gone through – and that changed our friendship. I remembered the coach journey to the *Romeo and Juliet* auditions just over a year ago. That seemed, now, to belong to another lifetime. Even then I knew I was different from Grace and Emmi. I'd wished for love. Deep, true love.

And I'd found it.

Grace had no idea.

After she and James had gone, I went up to my room. My thoughts, as always, turned to Flynn. He would have understood the darkness of my life at the moment. Maybe he was in that darkness himself. I lay down on our bed and curled up. The pain of missing him washed over me in waves.

It was as bad as it had ever been. My mind whirled with memories until I fell asleep, crying into my pillow.

27

Several long weeks passed. I went to school. I avoided people and got on with my work. The girls who'd been so eager to hear all the details of the party incident when I'd started back at Norton Napier now thought I was stuck up and unapproachable and cold-shouldered me.

Which was fine.

I didn't want to talk to anyone.

Of course, I had to talk, some of the time.

I talked when I was asked questions in lessons. I talked to reassure Dad I was fine. I spoke to Mum on the phone every few days, telling her what I was studying and how I was learning to bake at the commune. And I answered politely when the commune residents asked me things. I discussed homework with Leo, texted Grace from time to time and chatted with Gemma and Ros about recipes.

I even talked to my counsellor, Beth. She was

older than Sally, and really nice. I told her a little bit about how I felt. Not the worst of it but some. I think it was supposed to help me, to get it off my chest. But, talking to Beth, none of it ever felt real. I cried alone but I never cried when I was with her.

Night-times were the worst. Sometimes I would wake in a panic; other times I would wake still believing Flynn and I were together. Either way, as reality dawned, the terrible naked pain of being without him would swamp me, taking away all hope and all possibility of happiness. I would lie, clutching my little silver heart bracelet, barely able to breathe I missed him so much.

I rarely went out. Leo and I spent our free time talking about college and listening to music. He started reading to me again . . . he just walked in one night with *Jane Eyre* in his hand, and sat down at the end of the bed. I was pleased. I liked being around Leo. He never mentioned his feelings for me again and, after a month had gone by, I started to hope they had transformed into the same feelings of friendship that I felt for him.

When I wasn't pretending to be fine, or hanging out with Leo, I buried myself in my AS work and tried to keep my mind off Flynn as much as I could. Some days I'd forget about him for minutes at a time. Others he was with me every second, weighing me down, making every step, every word, an unbearable effort. I couldn't stand the thought that he hated me . . . that our love had burned away leaving only darkness and dust.

I checked my phone every day for texts, calls, emails and messages. And I scoured the front door-mat for post every morning.

Nothing.

I couldn't believe how easily and completely Flynn had cut me out of his life. And then one Saturday afternoon, the week before Christmas, the doorbell rang.

I opened up, expecting to see carol singers on the doorstep. We got loads of them: kids who only knew one verse of 'Away in a Manger' and who obviously thought the commune 'hippies' would be a soft touch for loads of cash.

Flynn's sister, Siobhan, was standing on the door-step. She looked gorgeous – all long legs and red hair shining in the sunlight. Her eyes widened as she looked at me.

'Oh, River.'

I stared at her, a million questions flooding my head.

Have you seen him?

Is he all right?

Where is he?

'Can I come in?' she asked timidly. She glanced over her shoulder at the 4x4 car parked on the country lane behind her. 'Gary's here. He's got a few errands to run for his dad's salon but he'll only be a couple of hours – can I stay while he does that? It's okay if not, I—'

'Of course, come in.'

She nodded, then turned and sped off to tell Gary. I watched him get out of the car as she ran up, then wind his arms round her, bending down to kiss her goodbye.

I saw couples all the time at school. Normally it was hard seeing people together but there was something so tender about the way Siobhan and Gary leaned into each other that was beautiful to watch.

As Siobhan ran back into the house, I said: 'You and Gary look happy.'

She blushed. 'We're getting married, actually.' She held out her hand and showed me the glittering ring on her finger.

'That's great,' I said. I was genuinely happy for her, for them. I took a deep breath. 'Does Flynn know?'

Siobhan tugged off her coat and scarf. 'Yes.' She looked at me, her eyes round and anxious. 'I didn't have your number but I knew roughly where the commune was so we drove up here . . .' She stopped.

It sounded like she'd made a special trip. 'You mean you came all this way?'

'It's no bother. Could we sit down somewhere?'

'Sure.' I led Siobhan into the kitchen. I was certain we wouldn't be disturbed for a while. Leo and Dad and several of the other commune residents were outside, doing pregnancy checks on the Jacob sheep. I was on baking duty. The loaves I'd put in the oven filled the kitchen with their fresh, wheaty scent.

'That smells good,' Siobhan said, sitting down at the table.

'Thank you,' I said. 'I only just started baking properly.'

We sat in silence for a moment, then Siobhan took a deep breath. 'He's back in London,' she said. 'I thought you should know.'

'Oh.' My chest tightened. 'Has . . . have you seen him?'

'Not exactly.' Siobhan made a face. 'His lawyer called Mum. She'd been going out of her mind because Flynn wouldn't say where he was living and Mum was all set to come over here from Ireland to look for him, then next thing the lawyer rang to say he'd been given a caution for an assault.'

'An assault?' I gripped the edge of the kitchen table.

Siobhan sighed. 'He decked some guy in a club last week. It sounds like he was massively provoked but you never know with Flynn.'

'Did you speak to him?' I felt sick at the thought of Flynn in another fight . . . of Flynn in a nightclub . . . of Flynn in London . . .

She nodded. 'Two days ago. I was so angry with him. I mean, he wouldn't answer Mum's calls and she was worried sick. In the end I texted him and told him he was breaking her heart and that if he didn't take the call I was about to make to him I would never speak to him again in my life.'

I stared at her, amazed that she'd been so forthright.

She smiled. 'So he answered, all annoyed with me for being so heavy with him. And I had a go . . . about Mum . . . about you . . .'

'Me?' I stared at her. Not for the first time I was struck by the way her nose was exactly the same shape as her brother's. What had Flynn said about me?

'I told him what your dad told Mum . . .' Siobhan's voice was soft and sympathetic. 'About you locking yourself away and how sad you are.'

'Oh.' A fresh wave of misery surged through me. I dug my nails into my palms to stop myself crying but everything inside me was churning over. Flynn knew I was heartbroken. I couldn't even begin to imagine how knowing that might make him feel. Would he even care?

'My brother's such an eejit.' Siobhan stretched out her legs.

'Did . . . did he say anything . . . about me?' My face burned with humiliation as I asked the question. But I had to know.

'No,' Siobhan said. 'He said something about how he'd trusted James, that was all . . . I don't know, it didn't really make sense. He did say that if I ever got the chance I should let your dad – and Gemma, is it? – let them know he was grateful they took him in.'

Dad and Gemma and James. He hadn't even mentioned me. I promised to pass on Flynn's message, then asked Siobhan for more information.

She didn't have any – not about Flynn, anyway. All she knew was that he was staying with someone from Goldbar's gym and would be there until the New Year. After that, she had no idea where he was going or what he was doing.

Siobhan talked for a little longer about her wedding plans – she and Gary were hoping to get married next summer, though she wasn't yet sure where. After a while, Gary returned to pick her up. I thanked her profusely for taking so much trouble to come and see me and asked her to say hi to her mum and little sister, Caitlin. I chatted and smiled as I kissed her goodbye but inside poison ran through my veins.

Flynn still hated me. It was obvious. He blamed and resented me as much as he had done the night of the party. He loathed me.

I loathed myself.

28

After Siobhan's visit, I stayed in my room again for two whole days. I told Dad and Gemma I wasn't feeling well. I lay in bed, agonising over what Siobhan had said. Nobody else understood or would ever understand.

I got up for Christmas Day and helped with the big lunch. I pulled my cracker, put on my paper hat and even managed a laugh at my stupid cracker joke. Dad was pleased I seemed so cheerful. I knew he was thinking maybe I'd turned a corner and was getting over Flynn. Stone was there too. I'd missed his birthday completely while I was so wrapped up in mourning Flynn, so I'd made a special effort with his Christmas present, asking Leo to help me choose some really stylish tops for him and putting them together with a proper skincare package. All dedicated stuff for boys. I'd seen Stone was trying to make an effort with how he looked and thought that maybe, as his big sister, I should try and help. He shrugged and grunted a 'thank you' when he opened the present but I could see he was pleased underneath.

After we'd exchanged all our gifts, Dad said he had something to tell us. He took me and Stone to one side and announced that Gemma was pregnant again. He explained they'd wanted to wait a full fourteen weeks before they said anything because of Gemma's miscarriage earlier in the year. He stressed Stone and I were the first people they'd told.

Stone didn't seem that bothered one way or the other but I was delighted. I gave Dad a kiss, then went to find Gemma to tell her how thrilled I was. Tears started into her eyes as I hugged her.

'And I'll be here to help when it's born,' I said, imagining how brilliant it was going to be to have a little brother or sister. 'When is it due?'

'The end of June,' Gemma said with a smile.

So the baby would arrive almost exactly a year after I'd come to live at the commune. It seemed a good omen. Dad said it was okay to let people know and the first person I wanted to tell was Leo. I ran to find him. He was down in the apple orchard, wrapped in two jumpers and a scarf, reading one of his Spanish lit books. His eyes lit up when I told him about the baby and I rushed back to the house full of excitement and hope, happier than I'd been in ages.

My good mood didn't last long. After our big veggie Christmas lunch, Dad drove me and Stone to Mum's and we had another meal with her and a couple of her friends that evening. Mum got on my nerves almost immediately, with comments about how I needed to put on some weight and get a haircut. I slept badly that night and woke late. After trying to force me to eat a cheese omelette for breakfast, Mum suggested we went to the Boxing Day sales that afternoon. I refused. Clothes shopping was the last thing I could face. Then she tried to get me to call Grace and Emmi. I couldn't believe she thought it would be okay for me to be friends with Emmi again – she knew enough of the story of the party night to be aware of how Emmi's revelation was the trigger for my break-up with Flynn.

'For goodness' sake, River,' Mum snapped when I challenged her. 'Emmi did you a favour. Can't you see that now?'

I said nothing. Mum would never get it. There was no point talking to her. Instead I got up, grabbed a jacket and headed outside.

It was a crisp, cold day and the chill wind bit at

my face as I strode angrily along the street. London seemed so small to me now . . . so cramped and dirty.

I wasn't really thinking about where I was going, I just wanted to get away from Mum, but my feet led me to Priory Park, where Flynn and I had met on our first date and so many times after. It was starting to rain as I wandered across the concrete playground, past the basketball hoops and along the path, up to the café and the open air paddling pool. Both were closed, of course. In fact, the whole park was deserted. The few people who'd been in here when I arrived, walking dogs or ferrying children to the play area across the grass, vanished as the rain grew heavier. Soon I was drenched, so I turned and headed for home.

As I trudged up the hill, the wind grew stronger. I bowed my head, spiky raindrops stinging my cheeks. It was still pelting down as I reached the top of my road.

'River!' It was him. *His* voice.

I looked up, my heart racing. I peered across the street, shielding my eyes against the rain.

He was standing by a lamp post on the other side of the road, his shoulders hunched against the rain. We stared at each other for a few seconds, then Flynn ran across the road towards me. I staggered backwards, my legs turning to jelly. I leaned against the cold, damp brick of the garden wall behind me as he slowed and stopped.

He stood half a metre away from me, his eyes fixed on mine. I couldn't speak, could barely breathe. He looked the same, yet different – his face was thinner and his hair shorter; there were lines under his green-gold eyes and I had never seen that trench coat before.

Rain trickled down his face. The world stood still. My hands shook. My body trembled. I couldn't think. I couldn't make sense of what was happening. All I knew was that he was here, really here, right in front of me.

'I had to see you,' he said.

I hugged my arms around my damp jacket, trying to hide my trembling hands. For a moment I thought I might actually be sick.

'I came here trying to get up the courage to come to your mum's house,' he went on. 'James told me you were here today. I saw you leave, I followed you all the way to the park. I watched you walk around, then when you started heading back here I . . .' He paused. A clap of thunder sounded in the distance. 'I wanted to say I'm sorry.'

I stared at him. *Sorry?*

'I shouldn't have run off like I did. I should have

said something to your dad. I should have checked Leo was all right instead of just calling the hospital the next day. I should have apologised for hitting him. I should have talked to you.' He fell silent.

I tried to process what he was saying but his words clattered around me, making no sense.

Thunder rumbled again in the distance. I shivered. Flynn took off his coat and held it out. He was wearing slim-cut trousers and a sleek, fitted top. They looked insanely expensive, as did the trench coat.

'River?'

I shook my head. Who did he think he was, turning up out of the blue and thinking he could just say 'sorry' and lend me his coat and that somehow the past two months would suddenly look different?

'I wanted to die,' I said, the words forcing themselves out through my chattering teeth. 'After you went, I wanted to die.'

Flynn came towards me, still holding out the coat.

'Please put this on,' he said. 'You're cold.'

Something in the gesture made me snap. Fury rose inside me and I lashed out, grabbing the coat from his hands and hurling it onto the ground.

'How dare you say all this now?' I shouted. 'How

dare you stand in front of me and say you're sorry after all this time and not speaking to me when I rang and rang and you *knew* how much I loved you and yet you still went and you stayed away and—'

'I wanted to come back the next day,' Flynn said, his eyes burning into me, his voice shaking with emotion. 'I fell asleep in a bus shelter just outside Norton and when I woke up I wanted to come back.'

'So why didn't you?' I demanded. The rain was easing now, the wind fading, but I was still shivering.

'What I said that night – most of it was an exaggeration but ... I didn't hate the commune but I didn't belong there either.' He paused. 'I hated all the rules, having to do all those chores.'

'I thought you liked the stuff we did, especially outdoors?'

'I did. It wasn't the work, it was being *made* to do it. Didn't you ever notice that though we were expected to do the jobs we were given, we never had a chance to join in any of the decision-making?'

I frowned. That was true, though I'd never thought about it before. All the adults on the commune came together for regular monthly meetings to work out what needed to be done over the next few weeks. Flynn and I had never been included in those.

'And then there was the counselling. The woman

I saw in London, before we went to live on the commune, was okay but I hated Sally and I hated those stupid group sessions.'

'So why didn't you say something before?' I asked.

'I did and they just said my "resistance" was all part of the freakin' process.' Flynn bent down to pick up his coat.

I glanced at his wrist. He was wearing a new silver watch. Where had he got the money for that?

'I wish you would put this on,' he said, holding out the coat again.

'What about me kissing James?' I went on. I was still angry but also shocked by how natural it felt to be standing here talking to him. 'How d'you feel about that?'

Flynn made a face. 'I was upset at the time but I realised afterwards I'd overreacted, as everyone who knew anything about it kept on telling me.' He rolled his eyes. 'James in particular. I called him the next day, ready to come over and fight him, man to man, but he was so furious with me, I . . . he told me to eff off out of his life, that I was stupid and cruel and . . . I couldn't believe it, that he had the freakin' nerve. So I left it, thinking he wasn't worth my time. Cut off all ties.'

'But you said you'd spoken to him – that's how you knew I was here.'

'I got back to London last week. It took me a few days but I went over to James's the night before last. I knew I had to apologise to him, too. Tell him I'd realised that the whole thing . . . the stupid kiss . . . was just a big nothing, really.'

I wiped the rain out of my eyes, barely registering that the drops had now stopped falling altogether.

'James is still angry at me.' He rubbed his forehead. 'Mostly about you. He told me I was an idiot and that you were still defending me to everyone, even though I didn't deserve it. Siobhan said the same thing.'

'Oh.' I realised I'd stopped shivering.

'That night when I left, it wasn't because I didn't want to be with you. It was . . . I dunno . . . it just hit me: I was living in a prison and I couldn't take it anymore, not the commune or the counselling or college. I was living this narrow life, somebody *else's* life. It was like I'd just woken up from a bad dream and realised wherever I turned I was just being pushed around, doing what *other people* wanted. I didn't even know what *I* wanted. I still don't.'

I stared at him, confused. 'I thought you wanted to go to law school. Don't you?'

'I don't know.' Flynn shrugged. 'I don't think so. Becoming a lawyer was always about *not* being my dad. Being the *opposite* of my dad. But I'm not sure if it's really what I want to do . . . who I am. I have to work out what *I* want to do. For *me*.'

'So you're not taking your A levels anymore?'

'Not right now, no. I'm earning money instead. Good money. I like it.' He sighed. 'How about you? Is college okay still?'

'It's fine . . .' I stopped. I wanted to ask Flynn about how he was earning his 'good money' but it was too surreal to have an ordinary conversation about everyday stuff with him.

'And Leo?' Flynn's face darkened. 'Has he asked you out yet?'

I thought back to the tortured conversation Leo and I had where he declared his feelings and railed against Flynn.

'We're friends,' I said.

'Ah.' Flynn hesitated. 'Look, I was right to leave the commune and try and work things out for myself but I wasn't right to do it in the way I did. That's what I came here to say. That it was all my bad. And that I'm truly sorry I hurt you.'

The skies clouded over again and the wind whipped up. He was saying he was sorry *I* was hurt. But it clearly wasn't the same for him. He had gone away and stayed away. He was fine without me. I was just part of a life he wanted to leave behind. I took a step away from him, feeling strangely calm. It was over. After all these months, it was over. The rain started up again, drizzling down our faces.

I looked down at my sweatpants and trainers. I knew my hair was plastered to my head and, in any case, badly needed a fresh cut, as Mum had pointed out to me several times since yesterday. I was wearing no make-up and my skin was grey.

I suddenly realised that none of it mattered.

'I miss you, Riv.' Flynn's voice was low and husky. He tugged the neck of his sleek black top to one side and drew out a worn leather thong. The tiny blue 'R' I'd given him dangled from the end. 'See? You're always with me. It hasn't gone away. I still love you.'

I met his gaze. 'But not enough,' I said.

'That's not true.'

'Yes, it is,' I said, feeling the truth of it deep inside me. 'If it was enough you'd have stayed. Even if you didn't want the commune you'd have found a way of being with me.'

Flynn shook his head. 'You still don't see, do you?' he said. 'I knew when I hit Leo I wasn't ready. I tried really hard to make it work. But loving you didn't make all the rest of it okay. And I . . . I love you too much to be with you when I can't be . . .' He tailed off. 'You can believe it or not but I'll always love you.'

The air froze in my throat. Rain spattered onto my

face. Flynn leaned closer, his eyes gleaming green in the sharp, early afternoon light.

Our lips touched – a light, sweet kiss like water on parched earth. I drew back.

'I have to go now,' I said. I still felt calm. Not numb. Not upset. Not even angry anymore. It all made sense, as if the world had shifted around me and I could suddenly see everything clearly.

Flynn loved me in his way but his way was limited. And I didn't have to feel bad about that.

I didn't have to feel bad about anything.

'Look after yourself,' I said.

Flynn nodded. 'You too.'

As I turned and walked away, the rain stopped and the sun came out, bright and brilliant, warming my face. I didn't look back until I reached my front door. Flynn was watching me from the end of the road. Tall and dark in his trench coat, the sun shone so fiercely that I couldn't make out the features of his face. I gazed for a moment at his outline, silhouetted against the steely sky. He raised his arm, casting a long shadow across the pavement, then turned and walked away.

I let myself into Mum's house. The smell of chips wafted towards me across the hall. My silver bracelet slapped lightly against my wrist as I took off my coat. I fingered the tiny heart then let it go and headed towards the kitchen, eager to get warm and to eat.

Flynn and River's story continues in
***Defy the Stars*, coming soon . . .**

Defy the Stars

Is this the end of the line for River and Flynn?

After months apart, everyone thinks that River
is successfully building a future without Flynn.
She has almost convinced *herself* that she is moving
on. And then, one day, Flynn is back, bringing with
him tales of his glamorous new life. River suspects his
lucrative new work involves some form of criminal
activity, but will she let herself be drawn back into
Flynn's world? Or is this, finally, the end of
the line for them both?

ISBN: 978-0-85707-105-7

ALSO BY

SOPHIE McKENZIE

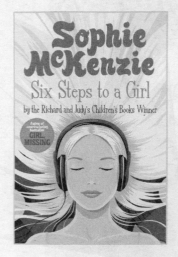

WWW.SOPHIEMCKENZIEBOOKS.COM

WWW.SIMONANDSCHUSTER.CO.UK

ABOUT THE AUTHOR

SOPHIE MCKENZIE was born and brought up in London, where she still lives with her teenage son. She has worked as a journalist and a magazine editor, and now writes full time. Her debut was the multi-award winning *Girl, Missing* (2006), which won the Red House Book Award and the Richard and Judy Best Children's Book for 12+, amongst others. She is also the author of *Blood Ties* and its sequel, *Blood Ransom*, *The Medusa Project* series, and the *Luke and Eve* trilogy. She has tallied up numerous award wins and has twice been longlisted for the Carnegie Medal.

@ sophiemckenzie_

www.facebook.com/sophiemckenzieauthor

www.sophiemckenziebooks.com